THE GREEN CHILDREN OF WOOLPIT

By Patrick Gunn

CONTENTS

1. THE LEGEND UNVEILED: ORIGINS OF THE WOOLPIT ENIGMA

HISTORICAL ACCOUNTS AND EARLY RECORDS

Long before modern investigations into unexplained phenomena, storytellers and scribes chronicled strange occurrences and unusual children, often in the form of rudimentary records or oral histories that later found their way into written accounts. Among these, the tale of the Woolpit children stands out as one of the most persistent and intriguing. The earliest mentions of their story come from medieval sources, primarily from the 12th century, that describe two children with unusual features appearing in the quiet village of Woolpit in England. These documents, though not written as scientific reports, provide invaluable glimpses into how such phenomena were viewed through the lens of that era. They often framed the children's arrival as a mysterious event, cloaked in folklore and local legend, yet rooted in real community reactions and observations. These early writings set the vibrant historical stage for subsequent interpretations and debates, anchoring the story firmly within a medieval context that saw every unexplained sighting as potentially linked to otherworldly phcnomena or divine intervention.

Medieval chronicles, often penned by monks or local historians, contain references, albeit brief, that describe the unusual appearance of these children, noting their strange speech, skin color, and unfamiliar clothing. The chronicles portray villagers' curiosity and concern, giving little doubt to the fact that something extraordinary had occurred. These records have been preserved through centuries, sometimes appearing in tax rolls, church records, or local histories, which, while not explicitly detailed with scientific rigor, suggest that the story was widely circulated and discussed among contemporaries. Such documents provide a layered account—combining oral tradition, local memory, and written records—that form the bedrock of what modern enthusiasts consider the earliest known evidence hinting at the existence of beings outside normal human experience. Their importance lies not simply in the facts they contain but in how they reveal the mindset and cultural context of the period, where unexplained phenomena were often intertwined with religious beliefs, superstitions, and local legends.

Scrutinizing the credibility of these medieval accounts requires understanding the cultural lens through which they were recorded. In the 12th century, many stories of strange children and supernatural sightings were often shaped by religious fervor, superstition, and oral traditions that blurred the line between reality and myth. Some historians argue that the Woolpit story might be a case of folk storytelling, perhaps exaggerated or misinterpreted by witnesses with limited understanding of unfamiliar or foreign customs. Others suggest that these early reports may contain kernels of truth —perhaps eyewitnessed events that have been embellished over time—that warrant serious consideration. The challenge lies in deciphering how much of the original record reflects actual events and how much is filtered through layers of storytelling and cultural narratives. For example, descriptions of the children's unusual speech or appearance could be based on genuine observations, but they could also be artifacts of local legend, exaggerated over generations. This analysis invites us to consider the possibility that these accounts may partially stem from misidentifications or societal fears, transforming normal strangers or visitors into mysterious beings rooted in local mythos.

Another key element is the origin of these reports—whether they stem from direct eyewitness testimony or later retellings. Medieval societies often relied on oral transmission, so stories could easily morph or gain new attributes with each retelling. It's vital to distinguish between physical evidence, which is almost nonexistent from that period, and the written descriptions that have survived, recognizing their potential biases. Some researchers posit that the reports may have been inspired by travelers, traders, or even children suffering from medical conditions like skin diseases or developmental disorders, which could explain their unusual descriptions. Skeptics often point to the absence of corroborative evidence and suggest these stories were misinterpreted or deliberately mythologized to serve moral, religious, or political ends. Nevertheless, whether myth or reality, these reports illustrate how early societies grappled with the unknown, attempting to reconcile extraordinary encounters within their worldview and cultural framework.

THE NAME AND LOCATION OF WOOLPIT

The village of Woolpit, situated deep within the English countryside, presents more than just a quaint historic spot; it invites curiosity through its unique geographical setting. Surrounded by rolling hills, lush fields, and a network of small streams, Woolpit's landscape seems ordinary on the surface, yet recent investigations suggest there might be more beneath its peaceful exterior. The area's natural features, especially underground formations and hidden caverns, have long fascinated those interested in strange phenomena. These underground spaces could potentially influence the local landscape, making Woolpit a site worth examining for any connection to unexplained or anomalous activity. The quiet, sheltered environment combined with the area's subtle geological peculiarities makes Woolpit intriguing for researchers trying to understand the wider context of unusual events reported nearby.

Looking closely at Woolpit's geographical position, the village lies nestled within West Suffolk, within close proximity to woodland and marshland. Such terrains are often associated with mysterious sightings, because they create natural concealment and complex pathways beneath the surface. The nearby earthworks and ancient riverbeds could serve as a backdrop for many local legends, possibly even influencing the physical landscape in ways that attract unexplained phenomena. People interested in UFO encounters and strange happenings find this setting particularly compelling, as the natural landscape itself might hide secrets—either ancient or alien—that are yet to be discovered. Sometimes, these geographical features can even distort signals or create atmospheric conditions conducive to strange light displays, which adds another layer of significance to Woolpit's landscape within the broader mystery community.

In terms of landscape, Woolpit's elevation and terrain create an environment where unusual sightings could potentially be explained by natural factors like magnetic anomalies, atmospheric distortions, or even underground influences. These physical features make it more than just a pretty village; they offer clues that could connect to the origin of strange sightings or incidents reported in the area. For example, reports of luminous objects or unexplained sounds frequently coincide with areas featuring underground water sources or mineral deposits, which can produce electromagnetic effects. For UFO enthusiasts and researchers, understanding these natural aspects can be a step toward deciphering whether Woolpit's landscape is a passive backdrop or an active participant in its mysterious reputation.

The name 'Woolpit' itself bears historical and linguistic weight, offering clues to its origins and possibly its role in local legends. The village's name appears in ancient maps and documents dating back centuries, often spelled in various forms such as 'Wolpit' or 'Wolpete.' These variations reflect the evolving language and settlement history, but also serve as markers that help tracing the village's past through historical records. By studying old maps, researchers gain insights into how the area was viewed centuries ago, and whether its name could be linked to myth or legend. Places with names that change over time often carry stories embedded in their words, sometimes connected to local folklore of strange beings, sightings, or mysterious events that might have shaped the village's identity over generations.

Historical map analysis reveals that Woolpit's location was strategically significant during medieval times, often positioned along trade routes or near natural resources. These maps not only chart the physical layout but sometimes hint at anomalies—such as unexplainable markings or symbols—that might allude to old legends of alien visitors or supernatural entities. The name itself may also have roots in old English words or local dialects, which could translate to descriptions of unusual phenomena or features associated with the land or its early inhabitants. For UFO enthusiasts, even the historical significance of place names, when correlated with reports of strange phenomena, can provide a layered understanding of why certain locations become hubs for unexplained activity and how their identities evolve over centuries. Examining these maps can help uncover whether the village's reputation is rooted in legend, real events, or a combination of both, adding a rich context for current investigations.

INITIAL SIGHTINGS AND WITNESSES

The first reports of the green children often come from quiet rural areas, where eyewitnesses describe vivid encounters that seem straight out of a dream or nightmare. In many cases, villagers report seeing strange figures near wooded edges or along lonely country roads after dusk. These figures are typically described as small children or young adolescents, with pale or greenish skin tones that stand out sharply against their natural surroundings. Witnesses frequently recall feeling a mixture of curiosity and fear as they observed these strange beings, noting their quiet demeanor and unusual clothing, which sometimes appears old-fashioned or handmade. Many reports mention these children speaking in a peculiar, hesitant manner—sometimes with no speech at all—adding to the sense of otherworldliness surrounding their appearances. Footage or photographs are rare and often ambiguous, but firsthand accounts remain the most compelling part of early sightings, fueling local legends and attracting the attention of curious investigators and folklore enthusiasts alike.

Among the most intriguing early witnesses are farmers, millworkers, and older residents who were often the first to spot the children at dawn or dusk. These witnesses detail how the children often appeared at the fringes of their farms or nestled within dense foliage, sometimes sitting silently and observing their surroundings. Several recount how, on approaching the children, the young beings would retreat or disappear suddenly, as if vanishing into thin air, leaving behind only faint impressions on the earth or strange, unexplainable marks. Some reports include descriptions of strange lights accompanying the sightings—a faint glow or flickering illumination that seemed to hover nearby—for which witnesses could offer no rational explanation. These early descriptions glue together elements of folklore, fear, and wonder, painting a picture of something not entirely human yet strangely innocent, which continues to fascinate those of us attempting to piece together a full account of these enigmatic encounters.

Additional witnesses often describe strange lights seen in the night sky surrounding the locations of these sightings. These lights are sometimes recorded as hovering silently or darting in erratic patterns, behaving in ways that defy known aircraft or natural phenomena. Witnesses who observe these lights often claim they have a strange, mesmerizing quality—bright, shimmering, and leaving a trail or flickering pattern behind them. Such reports add a layer of mystery, implying that the sightings of the green children may be linked to unidentified aerial phenomena, or possibly some form of cloaking or dimensional shift. Many of these firsthand accounts are supported by local lore and corroborated by nearby landowners or travelers who were in the area at the same time, creating a network of testimonies that offers tantalizing clues, yet still leaves many questions unanswered about what exactly was seen and how these initial sightings occurred.

The social and cultural climate of the time played a significant role in shaping how early reports were formed and interpreted. During periods when folklore and superstitions were deeply rooted in community life, seeing strange lights or encountering unusual beings often provoked fear or suspicion rather than curiosity. In isolated areas, stories of mysterious visitors or otherworldly entities could easily become woven into local legends, passed down from generation to generation. These stories were sometimes amplified by local gossip, religious beliefs, or even tabloid reports, which added layers of myth to the sightings. In some communities, these sightings occurred during times of social upheaval—such as periods of economic decline or political unrest—when people were more prone to interpret unexplained phenomena as signs, warnings, or curses. The cultural atmosphere also influenced the language used to describe these encounters; witnesses often employed terms like "fairies," "angels," or "spirits," which reflected the local worldview and belief systems of the time. Understanding this context helps researchers appreciate the subjective nature of early reports and recognize how cultural biases, fears, and expectations can shape accounts of supernatural or unidentified phenomena.

2. THE CHILDREN OF WOOLPIT: A DETAILED NARRATIVE

DESCRIPTIONS OF THE CHILDREN'S APPEARANCE AND BEHAVIOR

The children in question display an unusual and striking appearance that sets them apart from typical humans. Their most noticeable feature is their vibrant green skin, which appears smooth and almost luminescent in certain lighting, giving them an otherworldly aura. This pigmentation seems uniform across their bodies, without any visible variations or patches, suggesting a genetic trait that is unique and tightly linked to their physiology. The frail build of these children only adds to the mystery; their slender frames are fragile-looking, with delicate limbs that seem to lack the musculature and robustness common in children of similar ages. Despite their diminutive stature, there is a quiet resilience in their demeanor that hints at an unknown strength beneath their fragile appearance. Their features, such as slightly elongated fingers and large, expressive eyes, further reinforce their alien-like presence, making them resemble beings borrowed from a different world entirely. Many observers describe their movements as oddly graceful yet slightly hesitant, as if they are unfamiliar with regular human habits or confined by unfamiliar physical constraints.

The children often exhibit uncommon mannerisms, setting

them apart from ordinary kids. Their gestures tend to be deliberate, sometimes overly cautious, indicating that they might not have grown up with the same social cues or physical experiences as humans. They display a particular fascination with certain objects or surroundings, often reaching out with gentle, curious touches that seem more exploratory than playful. Their communication patterns are also unusual—some children tend to make soft, musical sounds, almost like a series of melodic chimes, instead of speaking clearly. When they do attempt speech, it's often in a melodious tone, sometimes with pauses that suggest they are processing unfamiliar sounds or ideas. They seem to harbor a remarkable calmness, rarely frantic or overly energetic, which could indicate a different developmental timeline or a different set of emotional responses. The children's unique mannerisms and physical traits evoke both fascination and concern, fueling speculation about their origins and the nature of their existence.

The behavior of these children reveals a mix of innocence and curiosity intertwined with subtle undercurrents of alien qualities. They tend to be shy around new people, often retreating into themselves or seeking shelter behind objects when approached by villagers. Still, once they become more comfortable, their gestures show genuine curiosity about the environment and the people they encounter. Despite their subdued nature, they exhibit moments of startling insight, observing their surroundings carefully and sometimes mimicking human actions with surprising accuracy. Their interactions with villagers are often marked by a cautious but persistent effort to communicate, even if their methods are unfamiliar or difficult to decipher. This can include pointing at objects, making gentle sounds, or engaging in silent gestures that seem deliberate and meaningful. Many locals believe that these children are trying to bridge the gap between their world and ours, even if they lack the words to articulate their intentions fully.

Dietary habits among these children are equally intriguing. They appear to have a limited range of food preferences, often focusing on fruits or liquids that are less processed or more natural. Some members of the village have observed that they prefer certain berries or sweet juices, consuming these in small, controlled amounts. Others note that they often avoid cooked foods or anything heavily seasoned, suggesting a possible sensitivity to taste or a different nutritional requirement altogether. This behavior might be indicative of a biological need to consume specific nutrients or a dietary pattern shaped by their origins. Their eating habits also seem to be deliberate—often eating slowly and with an almost gourmand-like focus—implying a different metabolic process or a conscious selection of what sustains them best. Observing how they approach food can offer clues about their physiology, possibly pointing to alien biochemistry that diverges from human norms. These dietary peculiarities deepen the sense of the children being from a different realm, not just superficially strange but fundamentally different in physical makeup and needs.

When it comes to social interactions, they are both fascinating and challenging. The children tend to form tight-knit groups, communicating among themselves in ways that appear instinctive and complex, yet difficult for humans to understand. They often display playful behaviors that are gentle and reserved, such as stacking stones, collecting shiny objects, or quietly watching villagers from a distance. Their responses to human gestures vary: sometimes they mirror actions, at other times they show signs of confusion or hesitation. Despite this, they seem to possess an innate sense of boundaries and patience, rarely forcing interactions or invading personal space. Several reports recount instances where villagers offered food or toys, and the children responded with subtle gratitude, reflected in their soft smiles or gentle touches. These interactions suggest possible recognition of kindness, even if their emotional expressions differ from ours. Their behavior points toward a worldview that might prioritize observation over direct engagement, reflecting a background vastly different from human childhood development.

Overall, these children continue to challenge conventional understanding, merging elements of innocence with unmistakable signs of alien biology and psychology. Their appearance, mannerisms, dietary preferences, and interaction patterns weave a complex picture—one that invites researchers and enthusiasts alike to question the boundaries between human and extraterrestrial life. Learning to interpret their subtle signals and behaviors could unlock vital insights into their origins and the broader questions surrounding unidentified beings from beyond our planet. A tip for observers: paying close attention to small, seemingly insignificant gestures or reactions can be revealing. Often, it's in these minute details that the true nature of their identity and intentions begins to emerge, opening the door to understanding enigmatic visitors like these children more deeply.

THE CHILDREN'S SPEECH AND LANGUAGE

When observing children or beings with unknown origins, one of the most striking features is often the way they speak. Their speech can be filled with unfamiliar sounds, rhythms, or accents that seem to defy typical human language patterns. These vocalizations may include sounds that are strange and unrecognizable, often combining elements that don't conform to any known language's phonetics. Observers might find themselves puzzled by how these children or creatures produce sounds that seem entirely alien, sometimes even adding peculiar inflections or intonations that hint at a different linguistic background.

This unfamiliarity can mystify both casual witnesses and trained linguists alike. Children or beings with otherworldly origins often exhibit speech that feels like a mix of tonal shifts, unusual consonant clusters, or melodic patterns that are difficult to categorize. These speech patterns could be rapid or hesitant, sometimes mimicking sounds from various languages, yet never fully aligning with any. This creates a sense of dissonance in listeners, as the sounds seem to exist outside normal communication. Their speech may also lack recognizable syntax, making it hard to decode any meaning or intention behind the sounds. This sense of mystery often fuels speculation about the origins of these speakers and whether their language is a form of communication from a different realm or dimension.

In some cases, reports describe children or entities whose speech appears to be a form of coded or encrypted sound. This has led some researchers to believe that their language may be based on principles entirely foreign to human cognition, possibly alien in nature. The unusual speech patterns are not just random noises but may serve specific functions, such as attracting attention, signaling distress, or communicating complex ideas in a manner incomprehensible to humans. Scientists studying these phenomena sometimes note their difficulty in even capturing accurate phonetic recordings, as the sounds may shift constantly or have layered resonances beyond normal auditory perception.

Many UFO enthusiasts and researchers consider the possibility that language differences could point to extraterrestrial origins. When witnessing children or unknown beings with speech that defies human language, some speculate that this could be a form of communication from other worlds. Unlike humans, who develop languages based on shared cultural and biological foundations, alien entities might communicate using methods rooted in entirely different sensory modalities. Their speech could be based on telepathy, vibrations, or other mechanisms that require decoding beyond traditional linguistic analysis.

This idea is reinforced by reports where listeners struggle to interpret the sounds, as though they are hearing a form of communication from a different dimension—one that operates on frequencies or concepts outside human perception. Some theories propose that these beings might be using a form of language that is not linear but rather multidimensional, with sounds serving as symbols for complex ideas or emotional states. Such communication could be entirely lost on humans because our brains are wired for specific types of language processing, making it impossible to understand without advanced technology or a new cognitive framework.

Throughout history, some individuals have reported hearing sounds or voices that seem to originate from extraterrestrial sources, often during close encounters or mysterious sightings. These experiences often include peculiar speech patterns that don't match any known language or accent. Some researchers hypothesize that in some cases, the language barrier experienced during these encounters could be a form of alien communication, intentionally designed to be incomprehensible to prevent human listeners from fully understanding their messages. Alternatively, it could be a sign of beings still trying to understand human speech themselves, resulting in distorted or broken language patterns.

For those exploring this mystery, a practical tip lies in analyzing these speech patterns not just as sounds but as potential signals. Sometimes, computational tools that analyze frequency, tone, and resonance can uncover hidden structures or patterns. These might reveal repetition or logic that isn't immediately obvious. Even more, researchers suggest attempting to identify universal aspects, such as rhythm or pitch shifts, which could carry meaning across different species or cultures, extraterrestrial or otherwise. Recognizing the limitations of human perception helps stay open to new ways of interpreting what may initially seem nonsensical, opening the door to deeper understanding of these unique linguistic phenomena.

THEIR INTEGRATION AND DISAPPEARANCE

The story of these children begins with their slow but observable entrance into the local communities that surrounded the area where many first noticed unusual phenomena. Initially, they appeared as shy, quiet newcomers who seemed to navigate the environment with a calmness that set them apart from other local children. Over time, however, the children started to participate more actively in community events, attending schools, markets, and festivals, gradually becoming part of the fabric of village life. Despite their initial differences—sometimes speaking in languages that locals couldn't understand easily or displaying peculiar behaviors—they eventually adopted local customs and routines, making their integration seem seamless at first glance. Yet, behind this seemingly smooth assimilation, there were subtle signs that their presence was unlike any other new residents, sparking curiosity and sometimes suspicion among residents who watched their subtle but significant transformation.

As years went by, records of their existence became increasingly sparse and fragmented, yet they persisted in some form within local memories and unofficial community notes. Schools occasionally noted the children in attendance, but their records would often lack complete details, as if parts of their histories had been deliberately obscured. Some residents and local officials who had interacted with them reported that their appearances seemed to shift subtly over time—features changing, accents morphing, or mannerisms subtly evolving—

making it difficult for even seasoned observers to keep track. Despite this, these children appeared to vanish gradually from official records, leaving behind only vague mentions in old newspapers or community stories. Their disappearance from documentation closely followed a pattern of them blending into the background, becoming indistinguishable from other children, almost as if they had been erased from official history while still lingering softly in the collective memory of the community.

Their final disappearance from the public eye seems to have been more than just a matter of losing official records—it hints at a deeper, more puzzling process. Some theories suggest that their absorption was part of a deliberate effort to conceal their true nature, perhaps linked to extraterrestrial or unidentified phenomena experienced in these areas. Others speculate that they might have been temporary visitors from another dimension or a hidden experiment that was discontinued. The sudden end to their visible presence raises questions—did they vanish because their purpose had been fulfilled, or was there some force that decided they should disappear before their true identity could be fully uncovered? It is this mystery that continues to fuel theories among UFO enthusiasts and researchers, who see their integration and subsequent vanishing as possibly connected to larger alien or unexplained forces operating behind the scenes. Tracing their footsteps offers insights not just into the children themselves but into the broader patterns that often accompany encounters with mysterious beings, who seem to fade into the background once their presence has served a specific, unknown purpose.

For those investigating such phenomena, a key step involves analyzing the patterns of their appearance and disappearance across different regions. Often, these disappearances follow a set sequence: initial emergence, gradual integration, and sudden vanishing often without trace. Recognizing these patterns can help separate purely folkloric accounts from more concrete evidence. Documenting timing, geographic locations, and interactions with locals can reveal overlaps with known UFO or paranormal activity in certain corridors. A practical tip for enthusiasts is to keep detailed logs of sightings and stories —such records compile valuable data points that, over time, might reveal connections that aren't immediately obvious. Since many cases involve inexplicable disappearances, understanding the contexts in which these children appear and vanish could uncover underlying mechanisms, be they technological, portal-based, or something else entirely. Remember, every piece of detail might be a thread leading to a larger picture, so meticulous record-keeping remains one of the most powerful tools in uncovering hidden truths about these extraordinary occurrences.

3. UNRAVELING THE MYTH: MEDIEVAL PERSPECTIVES AND INTERPRETATIONS

CONTEMPORARY MEDIEVAL EXPLANATIONS

Medieval villagers faced with mysterious phenomena often created explanations rooted deeply in their worldview, which was dominated by religion, superstition, and a limited understanding of natural laws. When unusual sights, sounds, or events appeared in the sky or on the ground, they were rarely seen as products of extraterrestrial activity or advanced technology. Instead, these incidents were woven into existing narratives that linked cosmic signs to divine messages, omens, or punishments. For example, strange lights in the sky might be interpreted as signs from saints or warnings from God, meant to instruct or chastise humanity. People believed that celestial phenomena had direct implications for their lives, often correlating them with biblical stories or moral lessons, which reinforced their worldview and provided a sense of understanding amid chaos.

Chroniclers and storytellers of the time played a crucial role in shaping these interpretations. Their records often exaggerated or fantastically described unusual events, adding moral or spiritual significance to them. If villagers saw a strange glow or a serpent-shaped cloud, they might record it as a manifestation of divine wrath or a herald of doom. These accounts served to explain the inexplicable and reinforce social cohesion by aligning extraordinary events with accepted religious doctrines.

Such rationalizations also offered a sense of control, as they linked unpredictable phenomena to familiar religious themes instead of randomness or cosmic chaos. In many cases, these explanations persisted for generations, coloring the collective understanding of strange occurrences long after the events themselves faded from memory.

Superstition and folklore formed the fabric of how medieval communities made sense of the mysterious. Ordinary villagers believed that certain animals, celestial patterns, or even unusual weather could foretell future events or reveal hidden truths. When strange aerial phenomena appeared, many saw them as bad omens or signals from supernatural forces. For instance, a strange bright light might be interpreted as the soul of a deceased person visiting the living or a warning of impending disaster, such as disease, war, or famine. Folklore stories, passed down through generations, often reinforced these ideas, describing dragons, spirits, or demons appearing in the sky or at night, symbolizing chaos or divine punishment.

Religious beliefs deeply influenced how these events were understood. Many saw divine intervention behind phenomena that modern observers might consider natural or scientific. Religious figures, from monks to bishops, would interpret extraordinary events as acts of God, either as signs of His displeasure or as calls to repentance. These interpretations served to remind communities of their moral responsibilities, often encouraging them to seek forgiveness or change their ways. In some cases, events like comets, eclipses, or unusual skies were linked to biblical prophecies or apocalyptic visions, heightening fears of judgment day. This blending of superstition, folklore, and faith created a complex web of explanations, making the strange seem both meaningful and inevitable within the existing spiritual framework.

On a practical level, these beliefs influenced everyday decisions, from rituals and sacrifices to pilgrimages and prayers. When

THE GREEN CHILDREN OF WOOLPIT

faced with inexplicable phenomena, communities would often organize prayer vigils, processions, or offerings, hoping to appease the perceived supernatural forces. These collective actions provided reassurance and a sense of agency, showing that even in the face of the unknown, familiar religious practices offered comfort. Recognizing how deeply these ideas ingrained themselves into medieval life helps modern researchers appreciate why alternative explanations like extraterrestrial encounters were absent from the period's narratives—reality was filtered through a lens molded by spiritual and cultural convictions, not scientific inquiry.

RELIGIOUS AND SUPERNATURAL CONTEXTS

Throughout history, many societies have sought to explain mysterious phenomena or unusual occurrences through the lens of their religious beliefs. During medieval times, children who exhibited strange behaviors or appeared in unexplainable circumstances were often interpreted as divine signs or demonic omens. Religious doctrines, deeply rooted in the worldview of the time, framed these children as symbols sent from heaven or as manifestations of evil forces. For example, a child born with unusual markings or exhibiting bizarre behavior might be seen as a vessel for divine messages or, conversely, as possessed by malevolent spirits. These beliefs didn't merely reflect superstition; they served as a way for communities to interpret the unknown through their spiritual filters, often leading to both reverence and fear. Understanding this context helps explain why reports of seemingly supernatural children were so prevalent and intensely scrutinized within medieval societies.

In addition to these religious explanations, supernatural and spiritual beliefs played a significant role in shaping perceptions of unexplained phenomena during the medieval period. Many believed that supernatural forces directly influenced daily life, especially in the absence of scientific understanding. Superstitions about demons, angels, spirits, and celestial beings permeated popular thought, providing a framework for interpreting bizarre or frightening events. Children thought to display supernatural traits—such as clairvoyance, prophetic dreams, or unusual physical features— were often seen as evidence of spiritual intervention. Society regarded such children as either blessed messengers or cursed beings, depending on the prevailing religious narrative. These explanations served to integrate the mysterious into a moral universe, where every strange occurrence could be ascribed to divine will or demonic influence, reinforcing societal norms and religious authority.

Furthermore, stories of children with supernatural qualities or divine signs were frequently intertwined with legends about angelic visitations, possession, or encounters with otherworldly entities. These narratives often carried moral lessons or warnings, reinforcing the community's spiritual values. For instance, a child who claimed to see visions or hear voices might be viewed as touched by angels or as a warning to the community about impending divine judgment. Conversely, if a child displayed violent or bizarre behaviors, they could be labeled as demonically possessed or cursed, leading to exorcisms or social ostracism. These interpretations reinforced a worldview where the boundaries between the physical and spiritual realms were fluid, and where unseen forces could influence human behavior and destiny. Such beliefs continue to echo in modern accounts of paranormal encounters, hinting at a persistent human tendency to seek spiritual explanations for the unexplainable.

FOLKLORE
AND CULTURAL
SIGNIFICANCE

Many stories told about strange lights, mysterious creatures, or inexplicable phenomena are deeply rooted in the local myths and legends passed down through generations. These tales often serve more than just entertainment; they are woven into the fabric of a community's cultural identity. In regions where sightings of unusual objects or beings have been reported for centuries, such stories reflect collective memories and shared beliefs that shape how people see the world around them. For example, in certain rural areas, tales of flying ships or glowing spirits have persisted for hundreds of years, becoming part of local traditions and rituals. These stories help maintain a sense of continuity, linking past and present, and offering explanations that resonate with the community's worldview.

This cultural narrative often elevates the story beyond mere folklore, making it a symbol of local history and identity. Some communities might interpret strange phenomena as signs from spiritual entities, ancestors, or divine forces, embedding these experiences within their spiritual practices. Others see them as warnings or messages that carry lessons about morality or societal values. Such stories can influence local art, festivals, and customs, reinforcing a sense of belonging and shared history. For UFO enthusiasts and researchers, understanding these cultural foundations is key to grasping why some sightings are so persistent and passionately believed, even long after the initial encounter. Recognizing these stories as part of a community's cultural fabric helps explain how certain phenomena maintain their significance over time.

Broadening the view further, these stories often mirror broader attitudes toward the unknown during medieval times. During this period, unexplained events, such as strange lights or celestial occurrences, were frequently linked to religious or supernatural forces. Medieval societies tended to interpret unexplainable phenomena within their spiritual framework, seeing them as divine signs or signs of divine displeasure. This attitude was reflected in legends and myths, where strange sights in the sky were often thought to signify gods or demons at work. The storytelling about such events served to reinforce societal norms and religious beliefs, as well as to explain occurrences that science had yet to understand. For individuals living in an era where natural explanations were limited, these stories provided comfort, order, and a sense of meaning—elements that resonate even today among modern UFO narratives. They reveal how cultural perspectives shape our understanding of the unexplained, linking myth and history in a continuous tradition of seeking answers beyond the obvious.

4. THEORIES AND HYPOTHESES: EXTRATERRESTRIAL ENCOUNTERS

ALIEN ABDUCTION AND UFO THEORY

Many researchers and enthusiasts have long debated whether unusual reports involving children might be linked to encounters with extraterrestrial beings. In some cases, children are described as appearing different after mysterious incidents, often with changes in their skin, eye color, or overall appearance that seem beyond the scope of normal medical conditions. These accounts raise questions about whether these children might have been taken by unknown entities, perhaps for experimentation or observation, similar to classic cases of alien abduction. The phenomenon often involves reports of children waking suddenly with no memory of what happened, but later developing unusual scars, unexplained injuries, or similar anomalies that cannot be easily explained through ordinary means. Additionally, stories sometimes include descriptions of strange lights or crafts seen in the sky near where the children were found or where incidents occurred, fueling the idea that extraterrestrial activity could be involved.

Witnesses and investigators suggest that these strange lights —often observed as bright, hovering or moving objects— might be directly connected to the abduction events involving children. Such lights are frequently seen in rural or remote areas where reports of peculiar sightings are more common. Some stories describe children who, after their disappearance or unexplained event, are returned with no memory but display physical signs suggestive of scientific tests or alien procedures. The consistency of reports across different regions and times hints at a pattern involving extraterrestrial entities potentially operating hidden operations on Earth, possibly targeting innocent children as part of their activities. While skeptics argue these stories are fabrications or misconceptions, the multiplicity and consistency of certain elements keep the mystery alive among UFO researchers.

The village of Woolpit has long fascinated historians and UFO enthusiasts alike, largely because of a legendary report involving strange lights and unusual sightings. According to local tales, in the 12th century, villagers observed bright objects moving erratically in the sky, accompanied by a series of strange noises. These sightings often coincide with times when unexplained phenomena—such as glowing lights or inexplicable crafts—are reported in the broader area. Some researchers have postulated that the legend of Woolpit's mysterious children could have roots in ancient encounters with strange aerial phenomena that predate modern records. The hypothesis suggests that these lights and sightings might have been early examples of unidentified flying objects, witnessed and remembered as part of local folklore.

Over the years, some have argued that these historical accounts could provide evidence of ongoing extraterrestrial activity in the region, possibly related to abductions or other encounters. The proximity of Woolpit to areas with frequent UFO sightings adds weight to this theory, especially considering the recurring themes of strange lights and otherworldly beings depicted in the legend. While skeptics dismiss these reports as natural atmospheric phenomena or misinterpretations of celestial objects, believers see them as clues lurking beneath the surface of folklore. The consistency of these stories across centuries may suggest a pattern of unidentified activity that has influenced local culture and stories, potentially connecting ancient sightings to modern theories about extraterrestrial presence on Earth.

INTERACTION WITH OTHERWORLDLY BEINGS

Many researchers and UFO enthusiasts have pondered the intriguing idea that some children, who report unusual encounters or vivid dreams of beings from other worlds, might actually be visitors themselves—either from distant planets or different dimensions. These young witnesses often describe interactions that feel surprisingly genuine, suggesting they might have experienced something beyond typical human perception. Some propose that children could possess a unique sensitivity or openness to these encounters, making them more receptive to subtle energies or signals that even adults might overlook. Others argue that children's vivid imaginations or lack of societal conditioning might lead them to interpret strange phenomena as encounters with mysterious beings. Regardless of the explanation, such reports fuel ongoing debates about whether these children are truly interacting with beings from outside our understanding of space and time or simply imagining these experiences due to subconscious factors.

One of the more captivating theories is that these interactions could be exchanges with entities from alternate dimensions —spaces that coexist with ours but are usually hidden from view. These beings might exist in realms stretching beyond the range of our senses, only detectable during specific events or states of consciousness. Children, with their naturally open minds and less skepticism, might be the first to perceive these entities or energies. Some accounts suggest that these beings could be travelers using advanced technology or dimensional gateways to observe or communicate with humans. Over time, accounts reveal common themes, such as seeing luminous lights, experiencing sudden flashes of knowledge, or engaging in inexplicable conversations, which hint at a deeper connection between children and these potentially otherworldly visitors. As these stories accumulate, they challenge traditional views about contact and demand a broader perspective that recognizes the possibility of multi-layered realities interacting with our world.

Many researchers believe that the key to understanding these visits might lie in exploring the broader nature of reality itself. Could it be that what children encounter are not just alien beings in the classic sense, but manifestations from a fabric of reality that we are only beginning to comprehend? This opens questions about consciousness, perception, and how energy could bridge different planes of existence. It's also worth noting that some encounters happen during altered states—dreams, meditation, or moments of heightened awareness—suggesting these interactions aren't limited to physical form but may involve consciousness directly. When examining these phenomena, it's useful to consider the possibility that these encounters serve a purpose beyond mere curiosity. They might be opportunities for learning, evolution, or even communication channels designed to bypass conventional understanding. Recognizing the significance of these experiences might lead to new avenues for scientific and spiritual exploration, offering insight into the true nature of what lies beyond our perceptions.

To explore these ideas more practically, consider observing children's reports critically but openly. Keep detailed records of their descriptions, noting even subtle details that might reveal a pattern or connection. Also, investigate whether certain environments or states of mind seem to bring about more encounters—such as during quiet, relaxed times or in specific locations. Such careful observation can provide valuable clues for understanding whether these experiences are conscious interactions or manifestations of subconscious processes. Encouraging children to journal their dreams and sensations might reveal recurring themes or messages that aid in deciphering the nature of their encounters. Ultimately, approaching these phenomena with both curiosity and skepticism enables a balanced investigation that can lead to a richer understanding of what these encounters might really signify.

EVIDENCE SUPPORTING ALIEN HYPOTHESES

Physical evidence and eyewitness accounts have long been at the forefront of discussions around extraterrestrial involvement. Over the decades, numerous reports describe objects with unusual flight characteristics, shapes, and behaviors that defy conventional explanation. For example, sightings of metallic craft performing sudden maneuvers, hovering silently, or accelerating at impossible speeds suggest technologies beyond our current capabilities. Many witnesses, including pilots, military personnel, and civilians, have claimed to see strange lights or crafts that appeared to defy gravity or physics, leading some to believe they are encountering something not of this world.

Some of the most compelling physical evidence comes from recovered materials, though definitive analysis remains elusive. There have been claims that certain metal fragments found at crash sites display properties not found in known terrestrial materials, such as being able to withstand extreme temperatures or exhibiting unusual isotopic compositions. While such claims are controversial and often dismissed by mainstream science because of the lack of peer-reviewed validation, they still fuel ongoing debates and investigations. Eyewitness testimonies tend to be consistent across different regions and times, with descriptions fitting patterns that seem too specific to ignore, such as the appearance of crafts with consistent shapes or behaviors that local legends and modern sightings mirror each other closely.

In addition to physical artifacts, we have a wealth of visual and sensory reports. Many are backed by photographs or videos, although some suffer from issues of quality or misidentification. Still, some footage shows objects that produce light profiles or flight patterns that appear impossible with known technology. Additionally, radar data captured during sightings has recorded objects moving in ways that contradict Earth-bound physics, often moving with high speeds, abrupt directional changes, or hovering in ways that defy aerodynamic principles. Collectively, these physical and visual testimonies form a growing body of evidence that many researchers argue cannot be easily dismissed as mere hallucinations, hoaxes, or misidentifications.

While skeptics point out the potential for misinterpretation or hoaxes, serious researchers advocate for a careful, open-minded evaluation of all claims. They stress the importance of corroborating eyewitness accounts with technological data, such as radar and sensor recordings, to build a more convincing case. Analyzing these incidents with modern forensic techniques can sometimes reveal telltale signs of technology far more advanced than ours, and perhaps even point to deliberate attempts at concealment or disinformation. Looking at patterns, locations, and consistent descriptions over years or decades might uncover a hidden truth: the lingering possibility that some of these sightings are direct encounters with alien visitors or probes from beyond Earth.

Modern technological data, including radar tracking and aerial surveillance, has played a critical role in validating or questioning eyewitness reports. When pilots or military radar operators observe unexplained objects on their instruments, it becomes harder to dismiss these sightings as simple optical illusions. For example, incidents like the 2004 Nimitz encounter involved fighter jets tracking fast-moving, unexplained objects on radar screens, which then performed maneuvers impossible for known aircraft. These radar traces often show objects accelerating rapidly, changing direction abruptly, or remaining stationary despite strong wind conditions—behaviors inconsistent with traditional aircraft or drones.

Advancements in sensor technology have steadily improved our ability to capture these phenomena, turning anecdotal sightings into measurable data. Often, these radar signals are supported by visual confirmation from military pilots or civilian observers, creating a multi-layered body of evidence. In some documented cases, sensors have recorded electromagnetic interference or unusual spectral signatures associated with these objects. Devices like infrared cameras, radiofrequency detectors, and kinetic sensors have been deployed at reported hot spots, revealing patterns that align with ancient legends describing mysterious lights and crafts. These modern technological findings deepen the mystery, suggesting that some phenomena may be linked to unknown propulsion or energy sources, possibly of extraterrestrial origin.

Lights in the sky often accompany these radar sightings, with patterns that cannot be easily explained. For instance, unusual luminosities or formations of lights—sometimes called ghost lights or fireballs—appear to move in coordinated manners or hover in place for extended periods. In some cases, these lights have been observed to emit pulses or change colors unexpectedly. When radar data confirms the presence of moving objects in conjunction with these lights, the case for non human technology becomes stronger. Such occurrences have been recorded worldwide, with reports coming from airfields, naval bases, and remote wilderness areas, where natural or terrestrial explanations seem unlikely.

One of the key features of these phenomena is their persistence over time and across different regions. They often resemble the descriptions found in folklore or early aerial sightings, strengthening the argument that these are not merely optical illusions or weather phenomena, but possibly signals or probes from intelligent beings. The consistency in the way these lights behave, combined with sophisticated radar tracking, paints a picture of objects that are not only real but potentially controlled by entities capable of manipulating physical laws. This collection of visual, radar, and technological data compels researchers to consider non-traditional explanations, leaning toward the possibility of extraterrestrial origins or unknown terrestrial technology that remains hidden from mainstream science.

In practical terms, for enthusiasts and researchers looking to examine or document such phenomena, it's crucial to gather multi-source data. Use radar devices if available, record visual sightings with high-quality cameras or phones, and collect environmental conditions during sightings. Cross-referencing all available data, documenting patterns, and sharing findings with credible organizations or institutions can help build a more convincing case. Sometimes, the smallest clues—like unusual electromagnetic signals or specific light patterns—can lead to breakthroughs. Maintaining a detailed log of sightings, even if they seem minor or isolated, can someday contribute to uncovering the reality behind these enigmatic events.

5. THEORIES AND HYPOTHESES: DIMENSIONAL AND PARANORMAL EXPLANATIONS

OTHER DIMENSIONAL BEINGS AND PARALLEL WORLDS

Many researchers and enthusiasts believe that some children who appear in strange circumstances may not originate from our familiar world at all. Instead, they could be beings from another dimension or parallel universe that somehow broke through the boundaries separating realities. These children often display behaviors or signs that don't quite match normal human development or history, leading some to speculate that they come from a realm where the laws of physics or biology work differently. Evidence for such origins is often anecdotal, but the consistent pattern of these stories hints at a deeper connection to unseen worlds beyond our understanding. This perspective suggests that our universe might be just one layer among many, with portals or gateways occasionally opening to allow passage for entities or travelers from other dimensions. These ideas challenge the very foundation of what we see as reality, opening questions about the existence of multiple layers of existence stacked within the fabric of what we call the universe. For some, this provides a plausible explanation for anomalies that cannot be accounted for by conventional science or history, giving fresh meaning to reports of children with unusual abilities or origins.

Exploring the notion that these children originate from other dimensions leads us into theories about portals, wormholes, and interdimensional travel, especially in cases linked to mysterious locations such as Woolpit. Wormholes are often depicted as shortcuts through space-time, allowing instantaneous travel between distant points in our universe. Some scientists and theorists believe that similar phenomena could connect our world with others, acting as gateways through which beings or information pass. In particular, the Woolpit incident, involving children found with green-tinted skin and strange speech, fascinates many because it hints at the possibility of a portal or dimensional rift opening nearby. These children might have fallen through such a gateway, emerging unexpectedly into our reality, only to disappear or be unable to explain their origins. The idea that natural or artificial wormholes could serve as bridges to other worlds is gaining traction among enthusiasts, especially when examining unexplained phenomena in remote locations that seem to transiently connect disparate realms. The presence of such portals could explain the occurrence of children or beings appearing with unfamiliar languages, appearances, or knowledge, suggesting their origins lie beyond our usual limits of understanding.

SUPERNATURAL PHENOMENA AND GHOSTLY ENTITIES

Many stories surrounding supernatural phenomena often begin with ancient legends that have been passed down through generations. These tales frequently describe mysterious figures or unexplained occurrences that seem to defy natural laws. In numerous cultures, such stories are viewed as evidence of spirits lingering from the past—ghosts of those who haven't found peace or have been trapped in a moment between life and death. These legends serve not only as cautionary tales but also as windows into a society's beliefs about mortality and the unseen world. When examining supernatural legends, it's crucial to consider how cultural context shapes these stories and differentiates them from modern interpretations of paranormal activity. Whether in folklore, urban legends, or personal accounts, many believe these ghostly presences act as messengers or remnants of unresolved conflicts, hinting at the existence of a spiritual realm that overlaps with our own.

Understanding these legends involves recognizing that they often reflect deeper fears, hopes, and societal values. Stories about spirits appearing during certain times—like nights during full moons or during specific festivals—highlight recurring themes of divine intervention or divine punishment. These narratives frequently feature spectral figures wandering in familiar settings, such as old houses, battlefields, or remote forests, fueling curiosity and fear alike. For many, these ghostly manifestations are seen as interactions with an invisible world that can sometimes influence the living, whether through subtle signs or startling encounters. The belief that such presences are manifestations of supernatural spirits is reinforced by stories of objects moving on their own, chilling cold spots, or unexplained sounds. These phenomena lead believers to interpret them as signs of spirits trying to communicate, warn, or enact revenge— a concept that has persisted across cultures for centuries. Often, these legends serve as a reminder of unseen forces at play and the mysteries still waiting to be uncovered.

In societies where these legends are prominent, rituals and customs have developed to appease or ward off spirits. This can take many forms—from offerings and prayers to specific rituals designed to cleanse a space of lingering energy. These practices reveal a common human desire to understand and influence the unseen forces around us. While skeptics regard these stories as mere imagination or psychological phenomena, enthusiasts see them as real glimpses into a supernatural causality that science has yet to fully explain. Some even argue that these stories serve as collective subconscious expressions of fears about death, loss, and the unknown. Whether one perceives them as genuine encounters or cultural expressions, these legends influence how communities perceive reality, shaping local folklore and ongoing supernatural investigations. For many, these tales act as a bridge between the living and the dead, offering a glimpse into a world just beyond the veil of our understanding.

The Woolpit area has long been a hotbed for reports of mysterious and unexplained paranormal activities that continue to intrigue researchers and enthusiasts alike. Local residents and visitors have recounted strange occurrences, from inexplicable lights flickering in rural fields to unexplained noises echoing through the night. Many of these reports point toward sightings of shadowy figures or strange figures that seem to vanish when approached. These encounters often happen in remote locations, such as old farmsteads, abandoned buildings, or near ancient landmarks that carry a sense of historical significance. What makes Woolpit especially compelling is its association with stories of otherworldly beings, which some interpret as alien or supernatural entities manifesting in this quiet countryside. Witness testimonies often include descriptions of feeling a sudden chill, a sense of being watched, or even brief contact with entities that defy natural explanation. Such reports have persisted for decades, reinforcing Woolpit's reputation as a place where the veil between worlds might be thinner.

Several specific phenomena have been consistently reported around Woolpit. These include unexplained luminous orbs floating across fields or above treetops, often observed during the twilight hours or late into the night. Some witnesses describe these orbs as moving deliberately, changing colors, or pulsating with energy—reminiscent of accounts from other regions where UFO activity is prevalent. Other reports involve hearing strange sounds such as near-human shrieks, metallic noises, or unearthly whistles that seem to emanate from nowhere. These auditory phenomena are occasionally accompanied by visual anomalies like flickering lights or brief, blurry apparitions. Despite the technological advances that have been applied to such reports, many remain unresolved, fueling speculation about the presence of supernatural forces, alien visitors, or residual energies lingering in the landscape. Researchers are especially interested in Woolpit because of its proximity to ancient sites, which may generate strange electromagnetic anomalies capable of generating these mysterious experiences. Collectively, these reports contribute to the area's reputation as a hotspot for paranormal activity, making it a prime location for field investigations and urban exploration for those keen on uncovering the truth behind these stories.

PSYCHIC AND HAUNTING THEORIES

Many researchers and enthusiasts have long considered the possibility that psychic phenomena can influence what witnesses perceive during unexplained encounters. The core idea is that certain individuals may possess heightened mental abilities, allowing them to access information beyond the normal senses. When witnessing strange lights or mysterious objects, these psychic actors might unconsciously shape their perceptions or even relay information that seems to come from beyond our understanding. Sometimes, eyewitnesses report feeling a sense of knowing or forewarning that aligns too perfectly with subsequent events, sparking speculation about the mind's role in interpreting and possibly manifesting strange experiences.

One common phenomenon in paranormal research involves people claiming to receive intuitive impressions at moments of heightened emotional or physical stress. This has led some to suggest that psychic energies or subconscious mind activity can influence perceptions, making witnesses more susceptible to seeing or hearing what aligns with their expectations or beliefs. For example, in cases involving UFO sightings, witnesses might interpret ambiguous lights or patterns as extraterrestrial based on their subconscious associations or pre-existing beliefs about alien encounters. Testing such claims becomes tricky because subjective perception heavily colors what is experienced, and often, these perceptions seem to be influenced by the viewer's mental state, cultural background, or even their desires.

Some researchers go further, proposing that psychic abilities could have a direct influence on physical phenomena during these sightings. They hypothesize that individuals with latent psychic powers may inadvertently cause disturbances or influence environmental factors, such as electromagnetic fields, which could manifest as unexplained lights or sounds. For example, if a witness unconsciously resonates with residual energy at a location believed to be haunted, their mental state might amplify or even generate visual or auditory illusions, creating a feedback loop that further distorts perception. This idea aligns with the concept that consciousness itself might be intertwined with physical reality in ways we do not yet fully understand, leaving open the possibility that human minds actively shape some unexplained phenomena.

Meanwhile, skeptics argue that many of these phenomena can be attributed to psychological factors such as hallucinations, suggestion, or cognitive biases. They point out that stress, fatigue, and expectation play significant roles in shaping perceptions of strange sights or sounds. For instance, in a haunting scenario, a person's belief that a location is haunted can lead them to interpret creaks and shadows as ghostly manifestations. This does not imply any real psychic influence; rather, it highlights how the mind, especially under certain conditions, can produce compelling but ultimately subjective experiences that mimic paranormal activity.

Thorough investigations sometimes reveal that eyewitness perceptions are heavily colored by personal beliefs, cultural lore, or media influences. Stories propagated through movies, books, or local legends can prime individuals to interpret ordinary phenomena—such as wind moving trees or shadows at night —as evidence of psychic or haunting activity. This interplay between perception and expectation is crucial for researchers to understand, as it demonstrates that human consciousness itself may have a significant role in shaping ghostly or alien encounters, whether through genuine psychic ability or psychological phenomena.

Some experimental attempts have tried to isolate psychic influence by using controlled environments and testing the ability of individuals to affect physical objects or electromagnetic readings. While results remain controversial and often inconclusive, these experiments serve to at least explore the possibility that mental states could have some influence on unexplained phenomena. For example, magnetic fields or static electricity sometimes spike during reported hauntings, but whether this relates to psychic activity or environmental factors remains debated. As such, the field continues to face challenges in providing definitive proof, but the notion persists that human consciousness could be a player in these mysterious events.

Turning to the other side of the discussion, claims of hauntings or residual energy paint a picture of places echoing the emotional or energetic imprint of past events. Many believe that intense emotions—such as fear, anger, or tragedy—can leave behind a lasting impression on a location, similar to how a photo captures an image. In this view, the 'residual energy' is like a psychic recording, replaying the emotional states associated with historical events, sometimes manifesting as apparitions, sounds, or unexplained movements. This theory is especially popular among those who study hauntings, as it offers a framework for understanding why certain locations seem to produce repeated phenomena without any current conscious intelligence involved.

Supporters of residual energy claims often cite cases where specific spots seem to 'haunt' multiple times, aligning with tragic or emotionally charged events from the past. Examples include battlefields, old hospitals, or homes where violent deaths occurred. The idea is that these emotional impressions are left behind like faint echoes, reactivated by environmental cues or the emotional climate of current occupants. Some researchers suggest that these energies are a form of subconscious imprinting on the surroundings, potentially influenced by natural electromagnetic or energetic fields that amplify these residual impressions, making them more noticeable to sensitive witnesses.

This perspective also ties into the concept that certain locations act as portals or recording stations for past energies, which may explain why the phenomena seem to recur in specific places and not others. It's important to recognize that this theory doesn't necessarily require an active intelligence behind the manifestations—rather, it posits that these are echoes of past events, triggered and amplified by current environmental factors. Understanding this helps paranormal investigators focus on the context and emotional history of locations, rather than solely attributing phenomena to discarnate spirits or psychic forces.

Many studies on hauntings emphasize the role of environmental factors such as electromagnetic anomalies, temperature fluctuations, and geological compositions in facilitating residual energy phenomena. Some locations with high electromagnetic fields, for instance, tend to produce heightened reports of apparitions or auditory phenomena. This suggests that residual or energy-based hauntings could be partly explained by natural conditions that influence human perception and possibly stimulate certain brain states compatible with hallucinations or illusions. By analyzing these factors alongside historical records of trauma or emotional intensity, investigators can piece together a more nuanced understanding of why particular sites seem to hold these ghostly echoes.

Whether viewed through the lens of psychic influence or residual energy, the idea remains that human perception plays a critical role in experiencing and interpreting the unexplained. Recognizing how expectations, emotional states, and environmental conditions shape these encounters can help enthusiasts develop more focused investigative techniques. For example, instead of solely relying on subjective reports, adding environmental measurements or psychological profiles to investigations allows explorers to better differentiate between perceived and actual phenomena. This practical approach enhances the chances of uncovering tangible clues while respecting the mysterious nature of these encounters.

6. THE GEOGRAPHY OF WOOLPIT: A LAND OF MYSTERIES

HISTORICAL LANDSCAPE AND ENVIRONMENT

The landscape surrounding Woolpit is rich with features that might explain some of the town's unusual stories. Its gentle hills, winding streams, and patchwork fields create a landscape that has been shaped over centuries by natural processes. These features aren't just pretty scenery; they could also hold clues to stories of strange sightings or mysterious happenings. For instance, certain hills and ridges align with ancient folklore, suggesting a long-standing connection between the land's shape and local legends. The town is nestled in a rural setting that invites exploration into how geographic elements influence both culture and perhaps even phenomena reported in the area.

Part of what makes Woolpit fascinating is how its specific geographic features could serve as natural landmarks or hideouts for unexplained activities. Its proximity to open fields and isolated spots might make it easier for phenomena to occur out of sight of everyday life. Streams and small lakes could contribute to mysterious sounds or lights seen at night, which some locals have reported over the years. Historically, towns like Woolpit often developed around easily defensible or resource-rich locations, and those same features could inadvertently contribute to the area's reputation for strange encounters. Mapping the terrain reveals patterns—such as secluded valleys or dense woodland—that could underpin stories passed down through generations, linking the land's physical layout directly to the town's legendary tales.

The underground characteristics of Woolpit offer another layer of intrigue. The region is known to have ancient caves and tunnels that stretch beneath the surface, remnants of old mining activities or natural formations. Some of these underground sites are vast enough to conceal hidden chambers or unexplored passageways. Such subterranean features create perfect hiding spots for mysterious objects or unknown entities, fueling speculation about hidden portals or secret bases in the area. People have occasionally reported hearing odd noises emanating from underground, which adds to the allure of these subterranean structures being linked to the town's mysteries.

Examining these formations shows that caves and hollow spaces often carry stories of unexplained lights or sounds. In some cases, local legends speak of strange glow or humming emanating from beneath ground, leading to theories that these could be entry points for otherworldly visitors or portals. Ancient underground sites also tend to be associated with archaeological remains, which some researchers believe could be linked to mysterious artifacts or symbols found in Woolpit's history. Due to their concealed nature and hard-to-access locations, underground caves become focal points for investigations into past and present phenomena. If you're exploring Woolpit's secrets, paying close attention to the area's underground features might reveal clues about potential hideouts or energy centers connected to unknown activities.

As a practical tip, creating an accurate, detailed map of local underground sites—noticing patterns such as frequent reports of activity near specific caves or tunnels—can help narrow down the areas most worth investigating. Equipment like specialized underground detectors or ground-penetrating radar can be useful for uncovering hidden chambers or anomalies deep beneath the surface, opening possibilities for uncovering concealed secrets in Woolpit's land formations and underground networks.

ALIGNMENT WITH OTHER UNEXPLAINED LOCAL PHENOMENA

The tales surrounding the village of Woolpit have long fascinated enthusiasts of the unexplained, especially when they are viewed through the lens of local sightings and strange incidents that share overlapping themes or occur in close proximity. Many researchers suggest that the mysterious story of the Green Children might not be an isolated legend but part of a web of unexplained phenomena that have persisted in the region over centuries. For instance, accounts of strange lights, unexplainable sounds, and unusual aerial activity often cluster around the same areas where Woolpit legends originate. These connections hint at a possible pattern: that the village's stories could be part of a broader spectrum of regional anomalies linked by underlying causes or shared origins drawn from ancient or ongoing phenomena. Notably, reports from local residents over the years have described sighting luminous objects or strange craft hovering near the countryside, sometimes coinciding with periods of heightened folkloric activity or mysterious disappearances. Such overlaps inspire questions about whether the legends are metaphorical placeholders for real events, or whether both stem from a common source—perhaps extraterrestrial or dimensional in nature—that manifests in different forms, depending on the observer's perception and cultural background.

When examining these links further, it's essential to consider the timing and geographic distribution of sightings in relation to documented legends. Historical records often show a pattern where reports of strange lights or unidentified craft emerge roughly during periods when stories like Woolpit's attain prominence or increase in local consciousness. In some cases, these sightings occur near locations with longstanding folklore of otherworldly beings, such as ritual sites or ancient landmarks that align with ley lines or energy grids. For example, a series of phenomenally bright aerial lights observed over the same hills reported in popular legend may signal a recurring electromagnetic anomaly or a deliberate attempt by unknown entities to communicate or observe the region. These correlations suggest that the legends serve as a kind of cultural map, offering clues to areas that might be significant in unexplained activity. Examining the similarities in descriptions, locations, and times allows researchers to see patterns that transcend individual stories, hinting at a regional pattern of unexplained phenomena interconnected by spatial and temporal factors.

Looking at the history of the Woolpit region reveals intriguing spatial patterns that may point to underlying anomalies or energetic hotspots where unexplained phenomena tend to concentrate. Over centuries, certain sites within the area have repeatedly been associated with strange occurrences—things like sudden drops in temperature, unexplained electromagnetic interference, or distinctive geometric alignments that defy conventional understanding. Cutting through layers of history, you might find that these locations—such as ancient burial sites, old stone circles, or natural formations—are linked to stories of strange lights, auditory phenomena, or even sightings of mysterious figures. These anomalies aren't random; they often display clustering in specific sectors of the region, which suggests that the environment itself may possess unique properties that attract or enable these phenomena. For example, some locations near ancient megalithic structures show a higher frequency of aerial sightings or unexplained sounds, raising questions about whether the ancient builders intentionally created spaces conducive to such activity, perhaps aligning with energetic ley lines or magnetic anomalies. Recognizing these spatial patterns helps form a clearer picture of how unexplained events are distributed and whether the region's physical and historical features contribute to these occurrences.

Further analysis of historical maps and recorded incidents supports the idea that the land itself might be a key factor in unexplained phenomena. In some areas, changes in topography, underground water flows, or geological compositions could influence electromagnetic conditions, creating natural 'hotspots' where strange events are more likely to occur. For instance, underground caverns or mineral deposits could facilitate unusual electromagnetic activity, which might explain sudden visual or auditory phenomena experienced by locals or visitors. Additionally, many of these sites are located along what could be considered energy pathways— like ley lines or geomagnetic alignments—potentially acting as conduits for otherworldly energies or phenomena. Mapping these patterns over time reveals a concentration of reports in specific 'zones,' reinforcing the idea that these places are more than just historical landmarks—they could be active nodes in a larger network of unexplained activity. Recognizing and understanding these spatial patterns could be a crucial step in identifying why certain locations act as focal points for strange phenomena and aid researchers in prioritizing investigative sites.

GEOLOGICAL ANOMALIES AND CLIMATOLOGY

Many locations known for strange sightings or unexplained phenomena are marked by distinct geological features that set them apart from surrounding landscapes. These anomalies often include unusual rock formations, hidden mineral deposits, or subterranean structures that defy normal geological processes. For instance, areas with highly magnetic rocks or unusual mineral compositions can create electromagnetic disturbances that might affect both human perception and electronic equipment, potentially contributing to sightings of unidentified objects or strange lights. Geologists and researchers have long studied these features, trying to determine if these geological quirks can generate electromagnetic fields capable of influencing human or animal behavior, or creating illusions that lead to sightings of inexplicable objects in the sky.

Unusual formations such as sinkholes, quartz-rich deposits, or mysterious underground tunnels often serve as natural spots for theories related to secret bases or hidden civilizations, which in turn fuel UFO and anomaly investigations. When these formations are coupled with anomalies like high levels of radon gas or strange soil compositions, they become even more intriguing. Some scientists suggest that certain geological structures may produce electromagnetic fields that could interfere with electronic systems or cause hallucinations, potentially explaining some observed phenomena. The alignment of these features with ley lines or other supposed energy corridors further adds to the sense that geology might play a role in shaping phenomena that defy straightforward explanation.

Another angle involves the ancient origins of some geological anomalies. Some sites with unexplained features date back thousands of years and are aligned with celestial bodies or ancient sacred sites. These connections provoke ideas that ancient knowledge or influence might have shaped geological formations, and that such formations continue to influence mysterious phenomena today. For investigators, mapping these features in relation to reported sightings can offer valuable clues, suggesting pathways or hotspots where activity is more intense. Recognizing the role of geology in these contexts doesn't just help explain phenomena, but also guides where to focus future research and exploration efforts, highlighting the importance of integrating geological surveys into anomaly investigations.

Climate and environmental conditions often shape local legends and stories linked to strange occurrences and sightings. Droughts, storms, unusual weather patterns, or even atmospheric anomalies can contribute to mysterious phenomena that are later woven into local lore. For example, luminous atmospheric events such as ball lightning or certain optical illusions caused by unusual temperature gradients can spark tales of visible craft or otherworldly beings. These environmental conditions tend to be transient but leave lasting impressions on communities, especially when sightings occur during specific weather events or seasons.

Environmental factors like magnetic storms, solar activity, or increased ionization in the atmosphere can also influence both human perception and electronic devices. During periods of heightened solar activity, for instance, radio waves and electronic signals often behave unpredictably, which might explain reports of strange lights or unexplained sounds. Similarly, atmospheric conditions such as fog, thin clouds, or dust particles can alter how objects are perceived, making mundane objects seem extraordinary. Historical accounts often link sightings or legends to particular weather or environmental events, hinting that some phenomena might actually be misinterpretations of natural occurrences amplified by the environment.

Understanding how climate has shaped local legend-building also involves recognizing how natural disasters or environmental upheavals can leave marks on collective memories. Earthquakes, tsunamis, or volcanic eruptions may have created strange sounds or lights that communities later interpreted as signs from supernatural or extraterrestrial sources. These connections are reinforced by the fact that certain sites with persistent legends are located in geologically active or extreme environments. By examining environmental data alongside historical reports, researchers can piece together a clearer picture of how nature influences human stories—offering possible rational explanations for phenomena that initially seem to defy natural laws. Recognizing these environmental influences helps trend investigators toward natural causes before jumping to more extraordinary conclusions.

Paying attention to atmospheric phenomena and environmental patterns is crucial for those studying unexplained sightings. For a practical tip, always record local weather conditions and atmospheric data during sightings or reports. Over time, correlating this information can reveal patterns that demystify many stories, turning initially baffling reports into understandable natural events. In the process, this approach helps refine the filters through which enthusiasts and scientists evaluate potential anomalies, ultimately sharpening the line between natural phenomena and true mysteries.

7. MODERN INVESTIGATIONS AND EYEWITNESS TESTIMONIES

CONTEMPORARY WITNESS ACCOUNTS

Recent testimonies from locals and researchers have added intriguing layers to the story of Woolpit and other similar phenomena. In the past few years, individuals living near the village have shared their encounters, describing strange lights in the sky, unexplained sounds, or odd sightings that defy rational explanation. Some locals recount hearing strange noises at night, which they couldn't identify—a mix of humming, clicks, or fleeting shadows darting across their property. Researchers, meanwhile, have conducted interviews with these witnesses, aiming to understand whether these reports are spontaneous reactions, misidentifications, or something that warrants deeper investigation. Collecting these firsthand accounts provides valuable insight into how events are perceived and remembered by those living close to the phenomena, helping build a broader picture of the current state of reports related to Woolpit.

One aspect that stands out in these accounts is their consistency. Several witnesses describe similar types of visual phenomena—flickering lights that hover or dart across the sky, often described as pulsating or changing colors quickly. Some report feeling an inexplicable sense of unease when observing these lights, as if something was focusing their attention elsewhere. Despite these similarities, discrepancies also appear, especially regarding the frequency, duration, and exact appearance of these sightings. For example, some witnesses recall brief flashes, while others report sustained glows lasting minutes. These variations could be due to differences in perspective, lighting conditions, or the natural misinterpretations of complex aerial movements. The ongoing collection of such accounts helps establish patterns, but it's equally important to recognize the diversity in individual perceptions and note the nuances that differentiate credible sightings from more ambiguous reports.

In addition, recent reports explore not only aerial phenomena but also encounters involving sensory experiences, such as feelings of being watched or sensations of temperature changes during sightings. Some individuals have described hearing unusual sounds—metallic ringing, low hums, or high-pitched whines—that coincide with visual sightings. Investigations into these reports often include recording devices, which sometimes capture anomalies that can't be immediately explained. For instance, a few researchers have documented unexplained electromagnetic fluctuations during sightings, adding a layer of scientific interest to the anecdotal evidence. Interestingly, some witnesses have linked their encounters to specific locations around Woolpit, with certain spots repeatedly cited as hotspots for these incidents. This pattern suggests that the phenomena might be localized or influenced by environmental factors, making them a captivating area for ongoing research and exploration of the unknown.

DNA AND FORENSIC ANALYSES

When scientists turn their attention to mysterious biological samples linked to UFO encounters or unexplained phenomena, they rely on a range of advanced techniques to identify and analyze these materials. Collecting credible samples is often a challenge because many reports are anecdotal and the samples themselves might be contaminated or degraded over time. Nevertheless, researchers use methods like microscopy, chemical analysis, and DNA testing to scrutinize the biological matter. Microscopy helps reveal cellular structures and possible contaminants, while chemical tests can measure mineral content, isotopic ratios, and possible synthetic residues. DNA analysis, on the other hand, aims to identify if the biological material originates from known Earth species or something potentially unknown.

One of the key steps in these analyses involves extracting DNA from the samples to see what creatures or organisms they might belong to. In some cases, sequences match known human, animal, or plant DNA, suggesting contamination or presence of common biological entities. However, when sequences fail to match any known species, it raises questions about the sample's origin. These findings can spark intense debates, especially if the biological sample shows signs of unusual properties like high resistance to degradation, anomalous isotopic signatures, or embedded alien-appearing cellular structures. Each of these aspects offers clues that could potentially support or challenge claims involving extraterrestrial or unidentified biological entities.

Evaluating such samples often involves cross-disciplinary collaboration—biologists, chemists, and forensic specialists working side by side. Despite sophisticated technology, the process is far from foolproof. Cross-contamination, sample mislabeling, and environmental factors can all lead to misleading results. This is why many scientific sessions on this topic include rigorous controls and repeated tests, sometimes with independent labs verifying findings. Often, results are inconclusive, leaving researchers with more questions than answers. Still, these efforts contribute valuable knowledge that refines techniques and builds a stronger foundation for future investigations into unidentified biological samples connected to UFO phenomena.

The goal of forensic studies in these cases is to piece together a credible, scientific explanation for the biological samples and their connection to unidentified flying objects or encounters. When results point toward known biological entities—say, human or animal tissue—it might suggest accidental or deliberate human involvement, contamination, or other terrestrial origins. On the other hand, if DNA sequences are ambiguous or unmatched, it can ignite curiosity and suspicion that there might be something truly unusual. However, scientists are cautious, acknowledging the limitations that make definitive conclusions difficult.

One major obstacle is the quality and integrity of the samples themselves. As biological matter ages or is exposed to environmental elements—light, moisture, heat—it degrades, making analysis tricky or inconclusive. Contamination from humans handling the samples or from environmental microbes can further muddle the results, leading to false positives or skewed data. Additionally, current DNA databases, while extensive, are not comprehensive enough to identify every possible organism or genetic mutation. This means that some sequences might genuinely be unknown, or they could result from mutation or hybridization processes that are rare or undocumented.

Another limitation is the difficulty in linking a biological sample directly to a particular incident or UFO encounter. Establishing provenance—proof that the sample originated at a specific site or incident—is often impossible without supporting physical evidence or eyewitness testimony. Even when a sample appears anomalous, the scientific community tends to remain skeptical until multiple lines of evidence align. This cautious approach stems from past cases where initial excitement gave way to explanations rooted in contamination, natural phenomena, or hoaxes. Therefore, while forensic studies can highlight intriguing features and narrow down possibilities, they rarely produce definitive answers in isolation.

Despite these challenges, forensic analyses serve as crucial tools for advancing understanding. They often act as a filter, helping to eliminate mundane explanations and focus attention on truly unusual data. Techniques such as mass spectrometry, radiocarbon dating, and advanced genetic sequencing continue to evolve, improving accuracy and resolution. When combined with careful field investigation and detailed witness accounts, this scientific groundwork can help create a clearer picture of what might be happening during these mysterious incidents. Ultimately, combining rigorous forensic work with open-minded inquiry provides the best chance of uncovering the truth or at least understanding what remains hidden beneath the surface.

A practical tip for enthusiasts and researchers alike is to maintain meticulous documentation of collected samples and their context. Knowing the timeline, environmental conditions, and handling procedures can make a significant difference in future analysis. Preserving samples in appropriate containers, avoiding contamination, and recording detailed observations ensure that if the materials are re-examined later, the data remains as close to original as possible. This approach maximizes the potential to decode clues that could clarify the nature of these unexplained biological samples or phenomena linked to unidentified aerial activities.

PARANORMAL INVESTIGATIONS TODAY

Woolpit, a small village in Suffolk, has attracted attention from paranormal enthusiasts and investigators for decades due to its rich history of unexplained phenomena. Recent investigations focus on reports of strange noises, shadowy figures, and sightings of mysterious lights around the ancient church and surrounding fields. Investigators often set up outdoor recording equipment at dusk, when activity seems to peak, to capture any anomalies that might occur during the night. Some teams have documented unexplained cold spots and sudden sensory distortions, which many interpret as signs of residual or active spirits. These investigations tend to be carefully planned, aiming to verify eyewitness accounts and gather tangible evidence to support claims of paranormal presence. Each investigation builds on previous findings, sometimes leading to the discovery of unusual electromagnetic patterns or subtle environmental changes associated with reported activity, which adds a new layer of context for understanding what might be happening in Woolpit.

To get reliable results, investigators often involve multiple methods, such as historical research to understand the area's past and its possible connection to the phenomena, combined with on-site recordings and real-time observations. The village's long history, including medieval legends and documented sightings over the centuries, provides a backdrop that fuels ongoing curiosity. Different teams employ a variety of tools —motion detectors, thermal cameras, and audio recorders—to scan for evidence. They sometimes set up long-term monitoring stations during quiet periods, hoping to catch hours of activity that might be missed in short sessions. Despite the variability of reports, the consistency of some phenomena keeps Woolpit high on the list of locations worth exploring in the realm of paranormal investigation. These efforts are driven by a combination of scientific curiosity and a desire to uncover what lies beyond our understanding of natural laws, making it a captivating case for anyone drawn to the mysterious side of life.

Modern paranormal investigations rely heavily on technological gadgets that help make sense of the inexplicable. Night vision devices are a staple for investigators working after sunset because human eyes alone have limited capability to pick up subtle movements or faint lights in darkness. These tools amplify available light, turning shadows and dimly lit objects into clearer images, but they can also sometimes produce false positives—like flashing spots or ghostly shapes—due to reflections or technical glitches. Still, when used carefully and in conjunction with other evidence, night vision can reveal movements or objects unseen by the naked eye, especially when investigators report hearing unexplained sounds. Electromagnetic field (EMF) meters are similarly popular, as some believe that spectral entities or residual energies can cause fluctuations in local electromagnetic levels. These deviations are recorded and later analyzed, though skeptics argue that natural environmental factors like power lines or weather conditions often produce similar readings.

Electronic Voice Phenomena (EVP) recordings have become a key part of investigations, capturing whispers, voices, or sounds that are inaudible during the session but emerge during playback. Investigators often leave recorders in areas where activity is reported, then listen carefully for any anomalies.

Sometimes, these recordings contain faint voices that seem to respond to questions posed by investigators, adding to the mystery. While skeptics see EVPs as simple auditory illusions or background noise, many paranormal researchers believe they could be communicative remnants of spirits. Both night vision and EVP recordings are tools that allow investigators to document phenomena over extended periods without disturbing the environment, which is crucial for capturing authentic activity. Their effectiveness hinges on proper usage; for example, keeping recordings free from interference and ensuring devices are calibrated correctly can make a significant difference in the quality of evidence collected.

8. SCIENTIFIC PERSPECTIVES AND SKEPTICAL ANALYSES

BIOLOGICAL EXPLANATIONS AND MUTATIONS

When trying to understand unusual physical traits in children that seem to defy typical human development, examining biological mutations provides a fascinating avenue. Some mutations occur naturally in humans, leading to rare features that might seem alien or extraordinary. For example, certain genetic changes can produce hyperplastic features like enlarged eyes or unusual skin textures, both of which could be mistaken for signs of alien genetics. These mutations often involve changes in genes responsible for growth, pigmentation, or tissue development. Sometimes, a mutation affects the process of cell division or differentiation, resulting in physical traits that stand out sharply against normal human variation.

One well-known class of mutations pertains to connective tissue disorders, such as Ehlers-Danlos syndrome, which can cause unusually elastic skin, hyperflexible joints, and unusual facial features. These traits, though rare, have been documented in medical literature and could resemble the descriptions of some enigmatic appearances attributed to unidentified children or smaller beings. Other mutations involve neural crest cells, which influence facial structure and pigmentation, potentially resulting in features that look otherworldly. These mutations may also lead to syndromes characterized by craniofacial abnormalities, which could be confused with evidence of extraterrestrial influence or hybridization.

In some cases, mutations interact with environmental factors or are complex, involving multiple genes. Such genetic shifts can produce diverse outcomes, from skin pigmentation changes to skeletal anomalies. For instance, mutations affecting melanin production can cause albinism, which leads to very light skin and hair, alongside ocular issues that make the eyes appear startlingly different. These features have fueled speculation about people with rare genetic backgrounds or mutations that produce strikingly unusual appearances. Documenting and understanding such mutations not only helps clarify biological variations but also assists researchers in ruling out non-human origins in reports of strange children encountered in anomalous settings.

Throughout history, many reports of strange children or hybrid-like appearances have been linked to environmental or nutritional factors that could alter physical development. During times of scarcity or specific geographic regions with unique environmental conditions, populations have experienced health issues that manifest in unusual physical traits. For example, deficiencies in essential vitamins or minerals—such as iodine or vitamin D—could lead to dwarfism, deformities, or abnormal bone growth, creating a distorted or exaggerated appearance that might be misunderstood as something extraterrestrial. These deficiencies often resulted from poor diet, contaminated water sources, or limited access to healthcare, especially in remote or impoverished locations.

Environmental exposure to certain toxins, pollutants, or radiation has also played a role in shaping physical anomalies. Exposure to heavy metals like lead or mercury, for instance, can cause developmental delays, facial deformities, or neurological issues that might be mistaken for alien features. Historically, populations living near industrial sites or exposed to radiation from nuclear testing or accidents have exhibited developmental abnormalities. These environmental factors can sometimes trigger mutations at the cellular level, or practical effects that produce visible anatomical differences, providing a plausible explanation for some reports of strange children seen in specific regions or times.

In many documented cases, community health crises or nutritional shortfalls lead to widespread malformations or health issues that resemble the descriptions given in tales of mysterious encounters. For example, outbreaks of congenital deformities during agricultural famines or war times often coincide with malnutrition and environmental stress, resulting in children with distinctive features that could be mistaken as evidence of alien intervention. Recognizing these patterns helps separate human-induced or environmentally caused anomalies from genuine unexplained phenomena. By understanding historical contexts and environmental impacts, researchers can better interpret reports and distinguish between natural causes and potential extraterrestrial explanations.

ENVIRONMENTAL AND GEOLOGICAL EXPLANATIONS

Natural phenomena often create conditions that can be mistaken for unusual or unexplained sightings. For instance, certain types of mineral exposure can cause surface reflections or glow, especially when exposed to particular lighting conditions. Some soils contain minerals that, when disturbed or heated, emit faint glows or shimmer, which might be misinterpreted as strange lights in the sky. Unusual soil conditions, such as high levels of phosphorus or arsenic, can sometimes produce luminous patches or strange visual effects that seem otherworldly but are rooted in geology. These natural emissions are often subtle but can appear extraordinary under the right circumstances, especially during nighttime or in low visibility situations. Recognizing these environmental clues requires careful examination of the terrain and a good understanding of local mineral composition, which helps differentiate natural glow from potential signs of something else.

Gazing deeper into natural explanations, geological activity plays a vital role in producing phenomena that could be confused with mysterious phenomena. Earthquakes, volcanic eruptions, and tectonic shifts create seismic waves and ground vibrations that sometimes generate auditory effects—rumbles, cracks, or deep booms—that are easily mistaken for unexplained sounds. These sounds are often accompanied by visual effects, such as flickering lights or glowing fissures caused by electrical discharges from stressed rocks or plasma phenomena within volcanic activity. For example, volcanic lightning occurs when ash clouds generate static electricity, producing brilliant flashes of light in the sky. These natural electrical discharges can resemble UFO sightings or unexplained luminous objects and are heightened during active volcanic periods. Understanding local geology and seismic activity can provide clues about whether such phenomena might be a product of Earth's internal forces, offering logical explanations rather than extraterrestrial hypotheses.

In some cases, geological processes generate localized atmospheric conditions that can lead to strange visual effects. For example, certain mineral deposits can cause mirages or optical illusions, especially in desert or arid environments. The interaction between temperature layers, humidity, and mineral-rich ground can create shimmering or wavering images —sometimes called superior mirages—that appear as objects floating or moving in the sky. These illusions are often mistaken for UFOs because they seem to defy normal visual expectations, but they are well-documented atmospheric phenomena based on light refraction. Similarly, ground-based electrical activity driven by mineral-rich soils or stressed rocks can produce faint electrical discharges that result in tingling sensations or flickering lights, further adding to the confusion. When investigating unexplained sightings, paying attention to the local geology and atmospheric conditions can often reveal natural explanations hidden in the environment itself.

To better differentiate natural from potentially anomalous phenomena, interested researchers should consider conducting simple environmental assessments. Checking mineral content in soil samples, monitoring seismic activity, and recording atmospheric conditions around the time of sightings can shed light on whether the environment itself could be producing observed effects. For instance, a quick soil test in an area with glowing patches or flickering lights might reveal high mineral concentrations prone to luminescence. Simultaneously, examining seismic records or volcanic activity reports can clarify if earth movements are coinciding with strange sounds or lights. By systematically analyzing the environment, enthusiasts stand a better chance of identifying natural causes, reducing misinterpretations and focusing on truly mysterious phenomena deserving further investigation. Always remember that nature offers a wide array of explanations, and understanding these basics can prevent jumping to conclusions about extraterrestrial origins that may not be warranted.">

PSYCHOLOGICAL AND SOCIOLOGICAL INTERPRETATIONS

Many times, what appears to be an extraordinary UFO encounter or a strange phenomenon can be explained through psychological factors like mass hysteria, hallucinations, or group suggestibility. When a group of people witness something unusual or hear reports about a strange sighting, their minds can become influenced by shared beliefs, fears, or expectations. This collective influence can lead to a situation where individuals start to see or believe in things that aren't actually there, simply because the group's suggestibility is heightened. For example, in communities where UFO sightings are strongly believed, eyewitnesses may unconsciously interpret ordinary lights or optical illusions as alien spacecraft, especially when reinforced by others' accounts. This phenomenon often results in a self-perpetuating cycle where stories grow more elaborate and convinced over time, driven more by psychological pressures than by actual occurrences. Recognizing these tendencies helps researchers differentiate between genuine encounters and phenomena rooted in the mind's tendency to fill gaps with imagined threats or sightings.

Understanding the social context is equally crucial when examining reports of unexplained phenomena. The environment in which reports are made can significantly influence their content and credibility. For example, during periods when UFO stories are prevalent in media or pop culture, people are more likely to interpret ambiguous stimuli as alien encounters, influenced by popular narratives and expectations. Social factors such as community beliefs, collective fears, or even local rumors act as catalysts that shape the way witnesses perceive and describe what they experience. Additionally, societal pressures or curiosity can lead to intentional exaggerations or embellishments in reports, especially in environments where such stories garner attention or fame. The influence of local authorities, media outlets, and social networks can also amplify or distort reports, often leading to a surge of similar stories that reinforce the initial narrative. By analyzing these social elements, researchers can better understand why certain phenomena are reported in specific contexts and how collective psychology can create a truth that feels real despite lacking physical evidence.

In practical terms, adopting a psychological and sociological perspective means looking beyond the physical sightings and considering how human minds and societal influences shape the stories we hear. For instance, in a small town where a few witnesses report strange lights in the sky, other community members might interpret the lights through the lens of local legends or media influence. If there's a history of UFO sightings or alien folklore in the area, new reports are more likely to mirror previous accounts, driven by the familiarity and suggestibility of the group. A key approach is to examine the timing of sightings and reports—do they cluster during media spikes or after specific events? This analysis can reveal whether collective psychology played a significant role. Ultimately, recognizing the power of suggestion and societal influences allows investigators to distinguish between phenomena rooted in the environment and those arising from human perception and belief systems. It's a reminder that sometimes, the mind's influence can be so strong that it creates the illusion of the extraordinary in a seemingly ordinary world.

9. THE ROLE OF MEDIA AND POPULAR CULTURE

DEPICTIONS IN LITERATURE AND FILM

The story of the Woolpit children, with their mysterious origins and strange green hue, has captivated storytellers for centuries. Over time, this tale has been woven into a variety of books, plays, and cinematic works, each adding its own flavor or interpretation. In literature, authors have often used the Woolpit story as a metaphor for the unknown, blending historical facts with imaginative elements to create captivating narratives. Some stories depict the children as visitors from distant lands, while others suggest supernatural or otherworldly causes linked to otherworldly portals or hidden worlds. These variations reflect not only the story's flexibility but also its deep appeal to those fascinated by the supernatural and the unexplained. When adapted for stage or screen, the Woolpit tale tends to emphasize its eerie and mysterious qualities, often overstating the surreal aspects to enhance dramatic effect. Writers and playwrights have used it to evoke themes of innocence lost, cultural clash, or even alien encounters, transforming it from a local legend into a universal symbol of mystery. For example, some modern novels have integrated the Woolpit story into science fiction plots, suggesting that the children might be early visitors or experiment subjects from an extraterrestrial realm. The adaptability of this story shows how folklore can evolve, inspiring new generations to view ancient tales through the lens of contemporary fears or scientific curiosity.

When it comes to movies, filmmakers tend to focus on the

visual and atmospheric elements of the Woolpit legend, creating haunting scenes that emphasize its otherworldliness. Many horror or fantasy films have borrowed elements of the story, portraying the children as enigmatic figures emerging from the shadows, often in foggy landscapes or ancient settings. This visual storytelling amplifies the sense of suspense and the uncanny, making it a powerful tool for evoking curiosity and unease in viewers. Some films present the children as alien beings, directly linking their green hue and strange accents to extraterrestrial origins, while others interpret their story as a supernatural event rooted in local folklore or myth. Playwrights, too, have adapted the tale for stage productions, using dialogue and staging to tease out the themes of innocence, separation from society, and the pursuit of truth. These adaptations often highlight how legends evolve over time, shaped by societal fears, hopes, and the desire for mystery. The creative reinterpretation of the Woolpit story in visual and theatrical media reveals its timeless appeal, serving as a canvas for exploring humanity's fascination with the unknown and the possibility of encountering the extraordinary in our own world.

Understanding how the Woolpit legend has been depicted across various media helps us see the story's broad influence on storytelling about the mysterious and the alien. Its recurring themes—stranger children appearing unexpectedly, their strange color, their awkward speech—are frequently borrowed when constructing stories about extraterrestrial encounters or supernatural phenomena. Creators often use this story as a template, adding modern twists or scientific explanations to suit contemporary audiences. By studying these representations, UFO enthusiasts can better recognize the symbolic language used in popular culture, which often echoes real-world questions about alien visitations and unexplainable sightings. As these stories have evolved, they have contributed to a wider narrative that blurs the line between myth and reality, fueling imagination and speculation. Recognizing these patterns allows researchers and enthusiasts to interpret new sightings or claims within a broader cultural context, understanding that stories like Woolpit serve as archetypes for humanity's ongoing fascination with the unknown. In practical terms, paying attention to how this legend is portrayed today can offer clues about public perceptions of alien encounters and help distinguish between fact and fiction when analyzing reports or witnessing unexplained phenomena.

UFO CONFERENCES AND DOCUMENTARIES

The tale of Woolpit has long fascinated those interested in paranormal phenomena, especially within UFO and investigation circles. Traditionally seen as a medieval legend about two children found in Suffolk with green-tinted skin and unusual origins, the story has been woven into modern discussions of mysterious entities and unexplained encounters. Investigators attending UFO conferences often bring up Woolpit as an example of how local legends can take on new life when examined through the lens of unexplained sightings or extraterrestrial theories. Certain researchers believe that Woolpit's story might encode hidden messages or signal ancient contact with otherworldly beings, making it a recurring topic during talks or panels dedicated to unexplained phenomena.

Many paranormal enthusiasts see Woolpit as a possible link between folklore and modern alien encounters. Some advocates suggest that the green children represent a type of strange visitor—possibly extraterrestrial or interdimensional—that somehow became embedded in historical narratives. These theories often revolve around the idea that such stories are not just myths but reflections of real, suppressed encounters with unknown entities. As a result, Woolpit frequently appears at gatherings focusing on ancient alien theories, time anomalies, or human-alien interaction. Its recurring presence in these forums fuels ongoing debates about whether traditional legends can serve as clues to understanding modern UFO sightings or encounters with strange beings.

When attending these gatherings, researchers and enthusiasts often exchange theories, comparing Woolpit's story with reports of bizarre creatures captured on video or eyewitness accounts that describe uncanny, otherworldly features. Some even suggest that the story's mysterious elements—such as the children's unfamiliar language and the green hue—align with reports of witnesses who describe luminous or colored humanoid figures. Woolpit's story is used as a bridge connecting ancient folklore with contemporary anomalies, making it a popular point of discussion among those trying to uncover the origins of unexplained phenomena. This blending of history and modern mystery keeps Woolpit firmly in the spotlight of UFO and paranormal investigation communities, often inspiring new hypotheses about the nature of the unknown.

Documentaries and media reports have played a significant role in shaping the modern perception of Woolpit, transforming it from a local legend into a subject of wider intrigue. Many television programs dedicated to the paranormal aim to connect Woolpit with larger themes, such as alien contact, hidden histories, or otherworldly mysteries. These productions tend to dramatize the story, emphasizing the children's unusual features, unexplained circumstances of their discovery, and the eerie landscape of medieval Suffolk. Occasionally, they integrate interviews with historians and folklorists, but more often than not, they focus on speculative theories that link Woolpit to extraterrestrial life or secret government experiments.

Media exposés tend to emphasize the more mysterious aspects of the tale, highlighting stories of strange lights observed in the sky near Woolpit during various periods, or suggesting that the green children might be remnants of a clandestine experiment or alien-infested journey. These portrayals often include reenactments, dramatic narration, and expert opinions that lean towards sensationalism. The goal is to captivate viewers and create a sense of mystery, which fuels ongoing interest and suspicion. The effect is a reinforced myth that Woolpit isn't just a story from the past, but potentially a glimpse into a hidden reality of unknown contact. This media framing influences public perception and keeps the legend alive in popular culture as a possible hint of extraterrestrial activity intertwined with historical events.

Many documentaries also explore the possibility that Woolpit may be evidence of an ancient alien presence lurking in the echoes of history. They analyze symbols, folklore, and archaeological sites that could possibly support this theory. For example, some suggest that the strange language spoken by the children might resemble an alien dialect or an ancient, forgotten one. While skeptics often dismiss these connections as fanciful, believers see them as intriguing clues that stimulate further investigation. Overall, media portrayals serve both to entertain and to push the boundaries of the traditional story, raising questions about whether Woolpit's legend is simply an old myth or a veiled account of encounters with beings from beyond our understanding. This blending of entertainment with speculation ensures Woolpit remains a fixture in discussions about the mysteries that lie just beyond human comprehension.

INFLUENCE ON
MODERN MYSTERIES

The story of Woolpit, with its bizarre tale of children with green skin and their mysterious arrival from an unknown land, continues to influence how people today interpret strange encounters beyond normal reality. For decades, this legend has been woven into the fabric of modern theories that explore the possibility of alien beings or creatures from alternate dimensions. Some researchers see Woolpit's story as more than just a local myth; they view it as a cryptic clue, hinting at ancient visitors who bypassed traditional notions of space and time. In this sense, Woolpit serves as a foundational myth that fuels discussions around the existence of beings from other worlds or realms that interact with our universe in ways we've yet to fully comprehend. Its enduring mystery encourages believers and skeptics alike to imagine a world where unexplainable phenomena are evidence of interdimensional travel or extraterrestrial contact.

In contemporary circles focused on alien encounters, Woolpit's story is often cited as an early example of a narrative that resembles modern descriptions of UFO abductions or alien interactions. Enthusiasts argue that the strange children might have been early interdimensional explorers or even entities from a different plane of existence who somehow crossed into our reality. This idea gains traction because Woolpit's tale, set firmly in medieval times, resembles many modern reports of strange beings emerging from unusual phenomena, such as light or portal-like structures in the sky. Some believe that

Woolpit's tale hints at ancient encounters between humans and beings that defy our understanding of genetics, physics, or local lore. Its relevance today lies in stimulating imagination and shaping theories that challenge the limitations of conventional science, pushing the boundaries of what might be possible within a universe full of unseen layers or hidden worlds.

The impact of Woolpit extends beyond just theories; it influences how stories are framed within the broader context of unexplained phenomena. Researchers and storytellers often position Woolpit as an archetypal example of a phenomenon that has persisted through history, bridging myth and modern mystery. Its story has been used to argue that evidence of alien or dimension-crossing entities has existed for centuries, disguised within cultural folklore. Films, books, and documentaries sometimes reference Woolpit as an ancient precursor to modern alien legends, creating a link that suggests that early encounters may have left subtle traces in our cultural memory. As a symbol, Woolpit embodies the idea that mysterious beings and their origins are woven into the human story, making it a compelling foundation for ongoing investigations into UFOs, portals, and other unexplained phenomena. This continued influence fuels the curiosity of both dedicated researchers and casual enthusiasts aiming to understand the unknown.

10. COMPARATIVE PHENOMENA: SIMILAR ENCOUNTERS WORLDWIDE

CASE STUDIES FROM AROUND THE GLOBE

Stories of strange visitors or mysterious children with unusual traits appear in many cultures worldwide, often sparking curiosity among UFO enthusiasts and researchers alike. In Europe, tales of children found in forests or remote villages who exhibit otherworldly features have circulated for centuries, sometimes described as having unnatural eyes or strange responses to human speech. Similarly, in parts of Africa and Asia, legends speak of young beings appearing suddenly in isolated areas, often with peculiar abilities or a lack of understanding of their origins. These stories tend to share common themes: small children appearing unexpectedly, often in rural or forgotten places, speaking languages unknown to local communities, or displaying strange physical characteristics. What makes these stories fascinating is that, despite originating from vastly different cultures and environments, they share recognizable patterns that point toward a possible universal phenomenon rather than isolated folklore.

Across these diverse stories, several elements tend to repeat consistently. The children often seem unusually alert, curious, or even frightened, yet they communicate in ways that seem beyond normal human ability—sometimes with telepathic impressions or expressions that suggest they come from elsewhere. Many witness accounts include children with features that defy typical biological standards, like glowing eyes, translucent skin, or unexpected physical behaviors. Another recurring element is the children's knowledge or awareness of things they should not have learned yet, hinting at an innate understanding or suppressed memories. Most intriguing is the pattern of their sudden disappearance after brief encounters or investigations, leaving behind questions rather than answers. These similarities hint at a deep-rooted connection that transcends geography and culture, raising questions about whether these stories are echoes of a larger, interconnected phenomenon involving unexplained visitors or entities linked to human history.

In examining these cases, some researchers suggest that they might represent a broad class of encounters with non-human entities, often associated with UFO activity and unexplained phenomena. These children could symbolize a link between the human world and something beyond what we understand, acting as messengers or indicators of larger cosmic or dimensional exchanges. For instance, the phenomenon of children appearing suddenly in the woods or fields coincides with sightings of strange lights or craft in the skies. Such overlaps strengthen the hypothesis that these stories aren't isolated myths but are part of a pattern involving mysterious contact or interaction with unknown intelligences. Recognizing these patterns helps enthusiasts develop a framework for understanding the larger puzzle, one that points toward interconnected episodes of unexplained occurrences across time and cultures, subtly hinting at a universal thread woven into the fabric of these stories. Paying close attention to these commonalities can help researchers identify recurring signs or signals that may lead to understanding the true nature of these encounters, whether they involve extraterrestrial visitors, interdimensional beings, or other undiscovered phenomena.

One practical tip for those studying such cases is to keep detailed records of local legends, witness testimonies, and physical observations. Many of these encounters happen in isolated areas where evidence can be overlooked or lost over time. By cross-referencing stories from different regions with similar core elements, it becomes easier to identify patterns or anomalies that demand further investigation. It's also helpful to document physical evidence such as unexplained markings, soil samples, or unusual electromagnetic readings, which could be linked to these mysterious children or visitors. When analyzing reports, paying attention to environmental factors—like weather, time of day, or nearby activity—can provide clues about potential connections to other phenomena. The recurring theme of children as symbols or catalysts in these stories suggests that researchers should consider the significance of innocence, vulnerability, and the unknown in their interpretations. By combining careful documentation with a broad awareness of cultural stories, enthusiasts can piece together a more comprehensive understanding of these universal patterns and their possible implications for unresolved mysteries of UFOs and encounters around the world.

CULTURAL PARALLELS AND DIVERGENCES

Across the world, cultures have developed their own unique ways of understanding and explaining bizarre encounters with unidentified phenomena. When a community witnesses strange lights in the sky or strange objects hovering overhead, their interpretations often reflect deep-rooted beliefs, cultural history, and social priorities. For example, in Western societies, such sightings might be viewed through the lens of technological anomalies or government experiments, often leading to interest in secret military projects or advanced aircraft. In contrast, many indigenous groups interpret these phenomena as spiritual signs or messages from deities, believing that such encounters are acts of divine beings or ancestral spirits trying to communicate. These contrasting perspectives shape the narratives around the phenomena, making what many see as alien ships viewed as sacred visions or supernatural events in different cultures.

Understanding how societies interpret similar phenomena reveals the importance of cultural context in shaping beliefs. For some, such encounters are warnings or blessings, often integrated into their spiritual or religious worldview. Others may see them as warnings of impending disaster or as testaments to unseen forces at play in their lives. This divergence isn't simply about different belief systems but also about how societies assign meaning to unexplained experiences based on their collective history. For example, in Japan, encounters with mysterious beings can sometimes be linked to folklore about yōkai or other mythical creatures, blending traditional stories with modern UFO sightings. Meanwhile, in parts of South America, sightings are often connected to legends of ancestral spirits or extraterrestrial visitors visiting sacred sites, blurring lines between legend and perceived reality. These interpretations influence how communities document, report, or even conceal these encounters, impacting the collective memory of unexplained phenomena.

Another key aspect is how media and popular culture weave these experiences into national or regional narratives. In the United States, UFO culture has become intertwined with notions of government secrecy and conspiracy, leading to a widespread perception that extraterrestrial visitors are hidden from public knowledge. Conversely, some African communities interpret unusual sightings as part of traditional cosmology, where spirits or ancestors are believed to manifest in unusual ways to communicate with the living. This cultural variance demonstrates that the same phenomena can evoke a spectrum of reactions—from fear and suspicion to reverence and acceptance—grounded in deep-seated cultural values and history. Recognizing these differences helps researchers understand that collecting reports of strange encounters should always be done with cultural sensitivity, as the way a community perceives and explains such events is shaped strongly by their unique worldview.

Cultures have long played a role in shaping legends and beliefs about strange encounters in the sky or on the ground. These stories are often passed down through generations, creating a tapestry of folklore that influences how individuals and communities interpret new sightings. Religious beliefs, historical experiences, and traditional stories all feed into the collective understanding of unexplained phenomena. For example, in medieval Europe, mysterious lights or flying objects were often associated with divine intervention or demonic activity, depending on the prevailing religious narratives. These interpretations served as moral lessons or warnings, deeply embedded in the spiritual fabric of society. Similarly, in societies with strong oral traditions, encounters with strange beings are woven into mythic stories that explain natural phenomena or serve as moral allegories, giving these stories a cultural significance that extends beyond the event itself.

Cultural factors also influence what details are emphasized or dismissed in the stories. In some cultures, the identity of the beings involved is central—are they gods, spirits, aliens, or mythical creatures? In others, the focus might be on the location or the timing of the event, linking it to sacred sites or particular celestial alignments. Social factors such as gender roles, societal hierarchy, and community cohesion also impact how stories are told and perceived. For example, women's accounts of encounters might be dismissed or interpreted differently depending on cultural attitudes toward female authority or credibility. Economic factors play a role as well; in regions where traditional livelihoods are threatened, stories of otherworldly visitors might be seen as warnings or signs related to environmental or industrial changes. These cultural influences shape not only the content of legends but also their purpose—whether to entertain, educate, warn, or reinforce societal norms.

Furthermore, legends and beliefs surrounding unexplained phenomena often serve as a mirror for societal fears and hopes. In times of political instability or social upheaval, stories of mysterious visitors might symbolize foreign threats or internal chaos. Conversely, in periods of scientific curiosity or technological optimism, such encounters are turned into intrigue about progress and discovery. These stories not only reflect cultural attitudes but also help communities make sense of unfamiliar or frightening experiences. When researchers approach these legends, understanding the cultural background is essential, as dismissing them as mere superstition ignores their deeper significance in shaping collective identity.

Recognizing how legends evolve and adapt over time also reveals changing societal values, making these stories more than just tales—they become repositories of cultural memory and insight into how people navigate the unknown.

SHARED MYSTERIES AND PATTERNS

Throughout countless reports and encounters, certain recurring themes seem to stand out among those who observe unidentified phenomena. Witnesses often describe seeing inexplicable lights moving erratically or in precise formations, creating a vivid impression that something beyond our normal understanding is at play. These lights can vary in color, intensity, and shape—from bright white or blue streaks to pulsating or flickering orbs—often appearing suddenly in clear skies or over remote areas. Many witnesses report them seeming to dance or hover, sometimes zipping away at impossible speeds, sparking curiosity and even fear. Noticing these recurring patterns helps researchers identify common threads that might point toward underlying causes or signals from these mysterious phenomena.

Beyond lights, details such as portals or gateways are frequently mentioned in sightings that seem to defy conventional physics. Some witnesses swear they've seen transverse openings—portals in the sky or on the horizon—shimmering and expanding before vanishing or revealing strange craft. Others speak of strange geometric shapes or shimmering curtains that seem to act as thresholds to other realms or dimensions. These features often appear in conjunction with the lights, suggesting they may be connected phenomena, perhaps some form of energy or consciousness projection. Recognizing the recurrence of such features fuels theories that the unknown might not be purely mechanical objects but interconnected phenomena involving space, time, and possibly interdimensional travel.

One commonality among many reports is that these shared features—be they unusual lights, portals, or luminous formations—often display some form of pattern or intentionality. For instance, lights tend to appear in certain configurations, sometimes forming geometric patterns like triangles, grids, or spirals. These formations are not random, but seem to follow specific arrangements, hinting that they could be messages or signals rather than simple visual anomalies. Similarly, portals or openings are often situated in specific environments—over water, in mountain ranges, or near unusual terrain—implying that certain locations might have natural or energetic properties conducive to the appearance of these phenomena. Recognizing how these features appear consistently across different reports suggests there are underlying rules or patterns governing their manifestation, which might unlock clues about what they truly represent or purpose they serve.

Examining the shared features across cases encourages us to look for connections that extend beyond isolated sightings. For example, lights that appear in clusters or rapid sequences might suggest coordinated activity, potentially hinting at intelligent origin rather than random natural phenomena. The recurring themes of shimmering gateways or geometric lights could indicate that these are not merely visual tricks but manifestations of some higher consciousness or energy form attempting communication or observation. It's also worth noting that these patterns often emerge during specific conditions—certain times of night, weather patterns, or alignments with astronomical events—indicating that some external factors might influence their appearance. By tracking these shared features carefully, enthusiasts and researchers can develop targeted strategies for observation, focusing on environments, times, and conditions that are most likely to produce meaningful sightings.

To make the most of these observations, keeping detailed logs is crucial. Documenting not just what is seen, but the environmental conditions and nearby terrain, can reveal valuable correlations. Over time, these patterns may help identify hotspots or cycles, offering a clearer picture of when and where these phenomena are most active. When approached with patience and attention to detail, uncovering shared mysteries can shed light on the possible purpose behind these recurring themes, guiding investigations toward deeper understanding rather than just superficial sightings. Remember, consistent patterns in the unknown may eventually point to a language or code awaiting deciphering—if we learn to recognize and interpret these familiar shapes and lights, we come closer to revealing what lies behind the veil of these enigmas.

11. THE PSYCHOLOGICAL IMPACT ON WITNESSES AND RESEARCHERS

TRAUMA AND MEMORY DISTORTION

Watching unexplained phenomena like unidentified flying objects or strange lights can have a profound impact on a person's mental health. For many, these experiences spark intense curiosity, excitement, or fear; for others, they may cause anxiety, confusion, or a sense of loss of control. When someone witnesses something that defies their understanding of reality, their mind tries to process this unfamiliar information, often leading to emotional upheaval. Over time, repeated exposure to unexplained sightings can create lasting psychological effects, especially if the individual feels isolated or misunderstood. It's not uncommon for witnesses to experience sleep disturbances, intrusive thoughts, or feelings of paranoia stemming from their encounters. In some cases, these unexplainable events can push individuals into states of heightened stress, which may develop into more serious mental health issues if not addressed properly.

Further complicating matters, the human brain is highly susceptible to influence and suggestion, especially when someone is unsure or highly motivated to interpret their experiences. Witnesses may find themselves lingering in a state of hyper-awareness, constantly scanning the skies or environment for signs of the phenomenon they saw. This hyper-vigilance can amplify feelings of fear or paranoia, leading to a loop where the mind's perceptions become increasingly distorted. It's also common for individuals to develop what is called hyper-memories, where their recollections of the event become emotionally charged, vivid, and sometimes exaggerated. These memories might be influenced by their emotional reactions, media portrayals, or suggestions from others, which can distort the original experience into a more elaborate or frightening story than what actually occurred.

Within the realm of trauma induced by unidentified phenomena, another challenge is distinguishing between genuine memories and those that may have been altered or fabricated. Trauma can cause someone to fixate on certain details, while neglecting others that might be less emotionally charged but more accurate. This selective memory often results in a distorted narrative that becomes difficult to untangle from reality. Some individuals may also develop false memories— recalling events that never actually happened—or believe they experienced something extraordinary when it was a product of imagination or influence. The brain's tendency to fill in gaps with plausible but inaccurate information can make it tough to separate fact from fiction, especially when someone has been repeatedly exposed to stories or images about similar phenomena.

Understanding that trauma from unexplained sightings can lead to memory distortion highlights the importance of approaching these cases with caution. Witnesses should be encouraged to document their experiences soon after they occur, preferably in writing or through recordings, to preserve unaltered details. Mental health support, especially from professionals experienced in trauma and suggestibility, can help individuals process their experiences more clearly and prevent their memories from becoming overly distorted. Recognizing the fine line between genuine memories and false recollections is essential for researchers seeking objective insights into these phenomena, as distorted memories can cloud the data, making it harder to uncover the truth behind the sightings.

INVESTIGATIVE CHALLENGES

One of the biggest hurdles in studying unidentified flying objects and related phenomena is obtaining data that can truly be trusted. In many cases, reports come from witnesses who might be influenced by fear, excitement, or even misunderstandings. Weather conditions, optical illusions, and technical glitches can also distort what is perceived or recorded, making it difficult to separate genuine anomalies from everyday occurrences or hoaxes. Researchers often face the frustrating reality that available evidence is incomplete, inconsistent, or simply not in a form that can be verified with certainty. Gathering reliable data requires meticulous attention to detail, skepticism, and a willingness to question initial assumptions about a sighting. Without this level of rigor, even the most compelling reports risk being dismissed or misunderstood.

Adding complexity to the challenge, many reports are influenced by biases and expectations — both conscious and unconscious — that shape how witnesses interpret their experiences. People tend to remember and describe what they expect to see rather than what actually occurred. For example, someone unfamiliar with typical UFO shapes might describe a strange object as a flying saucer, even if it was something entirely different. Media coverage also plays a significant role, exerting pressure on witnesses to interpret their encounters in sensational terms. When stories circulate about recent sightings or conspiracy theories, they can influence subsequent reports, leading to a cycle of false similarities and exaggerations. This interplay between perception, memory, and societal influence complicates efforts to establish a factual picture of what is happening in the sky.

For investigators, this means developing strategies to sift through the noise. Verifying witness accounts often involves cross-referencing multiple reports, analyzing physical evidence, and examining environmental factors. It's crucial to distinguish genuine anomalies from hoaxes, misidentifications, or optical illusions. High-quality photographic or video evidence, when properly analyzed, can provide tangible proof that supports or contradicts witness stories. Scientists and enthusiasts alike should remember that most sightings have logical explanations —yet, a small fraction remain unexplained due to the subtlety or rarity of the phenomena involved. Building a database of reliable data over time, with clear standards for evidence collection, can help uncover genuine patterns amidst the chaos.

To improve investigative accuracy, it's helpful to approach each report with a combination of healthy skepticism and open-minded curiosity. Fact-checking details such as location, weather conditions, and timing against known phenomena or aircraft traffic is essential. Recording precise descriptions and encouraging witnesses to provide physical evidence—photos, videos, or physical samples—can significantly improve the quality of data. Ultimately, the secret lies in developing methods to evaluate sources critically, recognize bias, and remain objective, even in the face of compelling stories. Remember that most myths and stories about craft in the sky are rooted in real experiences, but confirming what was actually witnessed is what makes all the difference in understanding these enigmatic events.

Practicing meticulous documentation and verifying information through multiple channels can drastically reduce the influence of biases and false reports. For anyone serious about uncovering the truth, keeping detailed notes, timestamping visual captures, and conducting environmental checks at the sighting location can provide invaluable context. This approach not only enhances the credibility of findings but also helps to build a more consistent picture of what is truly happening when something strange appears in the sky. It's often in the details—such as changes in altitude, movement patterns, or accompanying environmental conditions—that genuine anomalies reveal themselves. Staying grounded in careful analysis, rather than jumping to sensational conclusions, remains the most effective way to navigate the many investigative challenges that this fascinating pursuit naturally presents.

THE HUMAN MIND AND UNEXPLAINED SIGHTINGS

Many unexplained sightings of strange lights or objects in the sky can often be traced back to common psychological phenomena that affect human perception. For example, hallucinations are perceptions that seem real but occur without any actual external stimulus. These can be induced by various factors, including stress, fatigue, or certain substances, but sometimes they happen spontaneously, especially in individuals under emotional or mental strain. Sleep paralysis, another frequent explanation, involves a temporary inability to move or speak while falling asleep or waking up, often accompanied by vivid, sometimes terrifying, hallucinations of strange figures or lights. These experiences, though frightening, are rooted entirely in the brain's activity during disrupted sleep cycles. Cognitive biases also play a significant role; our minds tend to interpret ambiguous stimuli in ways that confirm pre-existing beliefs or fears, leading to sightings that feel very real but lack external evidence. The brain, seeking familiarity or pattern, fills gaps in perception based on personal expectations or cultural influences, making ambiguous objects seem familiar or extraordinary.

Understanding these psychological factors helps explain why many UFO sightings and unexplained phenomena remain unresolved. When people see lights moving in the sky or unusual objects, their brains attempt to make sense of these experiences based on past knowledge and mental shortcuts. For example, if someone strongly believes in extraterrestrial visitation, ambiguous lights might be instinctively perceived as alien craft, especially if their mind is primed to interpret strange sights this way. Similarly, during moments of fatigue or stress, hallucinations can be so vivid that they appear as real visitors or crafts, even though there's no external source. These insights emphasize how much human perception is influenced by internal processes rather than purely external realities. Recognizing that our minds can generate convincing but false perceptions is crucial for anyone exploring unexplained sightings; it reminds us always to question the immediate impression and consider psychological factors as part of the puzzle.

Many phenomena often attributed to extraterrestrial activity can be better understood through this lens. For instance, bright objects in the sky seen at night might be planets, satellites, or atmospheric phenomena like the Aurora, all of which can be misinterpreted during fleeting or ambiguous moments. People might also experience visual distortions when staring at rapidly moving lights or reflections, which can resemble craft or otherworldly visitors. Moreover, in the realm of hallucinations and sleep-related phenomena, some individuals report seeing beings or ships that appear to be real but are purely products of an overactive or disrupted brain. These experiences highlight the importance of considering psychological explanations before jumping to extraterrestrial conclusions. Being aware of how our mind works can help researchers differentiate between genuine unknowns and perceptual errors, sharpening the tools for investigating the truth behind these sightings.

For anyone interested in these phenomena, a practical tip is to pay close attention to the context of the sighting. Identify whether the observer was tired, stressed, or had recently taken any substances that might influence perception. Keeping a detailed diary of sightings, including environmental conditions, mental state, and other factors, can reveal patterns indicative of psychological influences. Recognizing the powerful role that internal processes play can lead to more critical assessments of unexplained events, preventing misinterpretation driven solely by expectation or emotion. If a sighting seems strange or convincing, taking a moment to analyze personal mental and physical states at the time can provide valuable insights into whether the experience might be rooted within the mind or potentially linked to external phenomena.

12. HIDDEN AGENDAS AND GOVERNMENT INVOLVEMENT

DECLASSIFIED UFO FILES AND SECRETS

In recent years, the release of government files has sparked a renewed curiosity about the true nature of unidentified flying objects. These documents, often kept secret for decades, have gradually been declassified, revealing striking details about sightings, encounters, and investigations involving unexplained aerial phenomena. Many of these files are compiled from military reports, intelligence agency assessments, and eyewitness testimonies, providing a layered view into what governments might have known and what they chose to reveal.

When examining these files, one immediately notices patterns—certain sightings show craft moving at speeds and with maneuvers that defy known human-made technology. Some reports describe objects cloaked in electromagnetic interference, causing disruptions in electronics and communications. Investigators often expressed skepticism at first; however, over time, accumulating evidence made dismissing these sightings increasingly difficult. The credibility of some encounters is reinforced by radar data, multiple witness accounts, and even physics-defying visuals captured on film or video.

Secret military bases, such as those in Area 51 and Dulce, feature prominently in these documents, fueling speculation about the importance and implications of fossilized discoveries. Many files mention sightings over restricted zones, suggesting an ongoing interest in studying or even reverse-engineering certain unusual craft recovered from encounters. Some declassified records go as far as documenting attempts to communicate with these objects or analyze their propulsion systems, hinting at a level of technological knowledge far beyond current human capabilities.

This body of declassified material has also shed light on government agencies' internal debates—whether these phenomena pose threats or are innocent anomalies. Some reports note aggressive intercepts by military jets, while others suggest possibility of surveillance by unknown entities. Over time, a consensus emerged advocating for transparency, leading possibly to future public disclosures. Such revelations offer a unique window into behind-the-scenes efforts to understand phenomena that challenge conventional science, often hinting at the existence of advanced, possibly extraterrestrial, technologies.

The intriguing idea that ancient legends might connect with modern UFO investigations has gained traction among researchers. The Woolpit legends, originating from medieval England, speak of two children emerging from a mysterious green-lit underground realm. The story describes their strange appearance, unfamiliar speech, and eventual integration into local society, fueling speculation about encounters with beings from another world or dimensions. Some theorists find compelling parallels between these ancient accounts and modern reports of anomalous beings and craft, suggesting a possible link across time.

Analyses reveal that legends such as Woolpit often feature themes of otherworldly realms, entities with unusual attributes, and unexplained phenomena that ripple through history. These stories might encode memories or cultural echoes of ancient encounters, which have been passed down through generations. When reviewed alongside declassified UFO files, some researchers speculate that the same or similar entities might have interacted with humans thousands of years ago, perhaps in hidden underground bases or in remote landscapes. Such connections challenge the idea that modern sightings are isolated events, hinting instead at a continuum of mysterious interactions.

Furthermore, the descriptions of beings from Woolpit—strange, sometimes luminous figures—resonate with many modern reports of luminous humanoids seen in UFO encounters. The underground origin stories resonate with theories that certain extraterrestrial or extra-dimensional entities might inhabit hidden subterranean worlds accessible to only a few. The consistent presence of such stories across different cultures and eras invites speculation that the boundary between myth and reality may be thinner than we assume. These connections open a landscape of thought where ancient legends and contemporary declassified files form parts of a larger, interconnected mystery that spans centuries.

It's fascinating to consider that these legends could be allegories or coded memories of ancient encounters, perhaps preserved by oral tradition to protect the knowledge from being lost or misunderstood. Some researchers argue that understanding these cultural narratives could serve as keys to deciphering the encrypted messages embedded in both history and modern sightings. Cross-referencing ancient stories with government files might reveal recurring patterns—geographical hotspots, types of entities involved, or even specific technologies—that could guide current investigations. By looking at these stories not just as myths but as cultural records, enthusiasts may uncover hidden connections that inform the ongoing search for truth about UFOs and mysterious phenomena.

Additionally, developing an awareness of these potential links encourages a broader perspective. It ventures beyond the confines of conventional science and explores the possibility of persistent, ancient interactions between humans and unknown entities. Such insights can inspire new hypotheses—such as underground bases that link ancient and modern encounters or the idea that some ancient legends encode knowledge of technologies or beings still lurking within the planet's hidden realms. Keeping an open mind, while critical and analytical, enables enthusiasts to piece together clues that span centuries, potentially unifying historical mythologies with evidence from current declassified information, creating a richer understanding of our mysterious universe.

GOVERNMENT COVER-UPS AND DISINFORMATION

Throughout history, many researchers and UFO enthusiasts believe that governments have intentionally suppressed or hidden evidence related to unexplained aerial phenomena. These theories often suggest that authorities possess classified materials or knowledge about extraterrestrial encounters but choose to keep them secret for reasons that range from national security to protecting the public from potential fear or chaos. For example, some claim that official reports of strange sightings and encounters have been dismissed or classified, preventing access to potentially revealing information. These narratives are fueled by leaked documents, whistleblower testimonies, and mysterious disappearances of data from public archives. Skeptics argue that many such claims are based on conjecture or misinterpretation, but the persistent pattern of secrecy has helped sustain suspicion that the government is hiding something significant about UFOs. The idea that powerful entities might suppress evidence fits into a broader pattern where authority figures often control what information reaches the public, especially when that information could challenge accepted scientific or political narratives.

Disinformation campaigns, whether orchestrated consciously or as a result of bureaucratic complacency, seem to serve a dual purpose. They can obscure genuine mysteries while simultaneously feeding misconceptions and false leads. Disinformation might take the form of fake leaks, planted stories, or discrediting witnesses who come forward with unusual sightings. Over time, such tactics erode trust in official channels, leading enthusiasts to question everything from government statements to mainstream media reports. When natural phenomena or technological anomalies are reported, authorities might release confusing or contradictory explanations, sowing doubt and muddying the waters about what is real. These actions can help keep sensitive information out of the public eye, ensuring that even when credible evidence surfaces, it is dismissed as part of hoaxes or misinformation. For many researchers, understanding this history of deception is crucial because it highlights the importance of verifying sources and critically evaluating official statements against independent data and eyewitness reports.

In many cases, the line between legitimate investigation and deliberate disinformation becomes blurred. There are documented instances where governments have benefited from spreading false narratives, either to divert attention from embarrassing incidents or to tame the public's curiosity about the unknown. In some cases, false information has been strategically used to discredit whistleblowers or credible witnesses, labeling them as conspiracy theorists or fabricators. Patterns also suggest that when genuine discoveries are made, they are often quickly overshadowed by sensational false stories designed to redirect public focus or create confusion. For enthusiasts, recognizing the signs of disinformation involves scrutinizing sources, cross-referencing reports from different agencies or independent researchers, and being wary of overly sensational claims. A practical approach involves maintaining a skeptical mind but remaining open to new evidence, as genuine disclosures can sometimes slip through the cracks of elaborate cover-ups.

Because disinformation relies heavily on misinformation, it's worth bearing in mind that many unverified reports or rumors, even if seemingly credible, should be examined carefully. Sometimes, what appears to be an official cover-up might be a result of bureaucratic mistakes or accidental data loss rather than deliberate deception. Yet, the persistence of secrecy, combined with unexplained data gaps, tends to reinforce the belief that not all is being revealed. For those researching this field, it's helpful to develop a habit of asking critical questions: Who benefits from suppressing this information? What is the motive behind withholding certain data? What independent evidence exists that could challenge the official story? These questions help sift through the layers of disinformation and potentially uncover genuine anomalies worth investigating further.

As a practical tip, always keep a detailed record of your sources and cross-check claims from multiple perspectives. For instance, if a report mentions a particular sighting, look for corroborating witness statements, declassified documents, or independent investigations. When faced with official denials or conflicting reports, seek data from open sources or expert analyses that haven't been influenced by governmental or institutional agendas. This approach aids in separating plausible facts from manipulated narratives, empowering researchers and enthusiasts alike to navigate carefully through a landscape filled with half-truths and intentional deceptions. The more diligent your verification process, the better your chances of distinguishing genuine anomalies from carefully crafted disinformation.">

MILITARY AND SCIENTIFIC INTERESTS

Throughout history, governments and military organizations have often shown a keen interest in unexplained land anomalies, particularly those that defy conventional understanding of geology, physics, or geography. Such anomalies might include strange land formations, inexplicable magnetic surges, or mysterious structures hidden within remote regions. These phenomena can intrigue scientific communities and military agencies alike, suggesting that they may hold secrets related to advanced technology, clandestine experimentation, or even undiscovered natural processes. The drive to explore these anomalies is often fueled by a desire to gain strategic advantages, secure borders, or uncover potential threats that could impact national security. Because of this, many unexplained land features are subjected to discreet investigations, often shrouded in secrecy to prevent public awareness of what might be discovered.

Military research, in particular, has historically sought to understand and control anomalous land phenomena that can affect communication systems, navigation, or security infrastructure. From magnetic anomalies disrupting compasses to land formations that seem to appear and vanish, the military has invested resources into studying how these irregularities can be weaponized or mitigated. Some theories propose that certain land anomalies might serve as portals or gateways to other dimensions, sparking classified scientific efforts to understand their true nature. For example, remote sensing technology and ground-penetrating radar are often employed in secret investigations to map and analyze these mysterious features without revealing their true purpose. In some cases, the evidence points toward experiments with energy fields or advanced materials that could be linked to clandestine projects aimed at developing next-generation technology.

Examples from various countries suggest that governments have a long-standing fascination with anomalies related to strange land formations. For instance, military documents have hinted at investigations around peculiar hills, sinkholes, or electromagnetic hotspots that align with reports of unidentified flying objects or strange sightings. These efforts are rarely acknowledged publicly but are often suspected by researchers who analyze patterns of unexplained activity in specific locations. The overarching motive appears to stem from a mixture of curiosity, strategic necessity, and a desire to keep potentially disruptive discoveries out of public reach. By controlling information about these land anomalies, authorities may aim to prevent panic, limit foreign intelligence access, or ensure that any technological advancements remain classified, reinforcing the idea that many mysterious lands are closely linked to state-sponsored scientific endeavors.

Moving into the realm of more speculative theories, some believe that secret investigations extend beyond purely natural anomalies and into the realm of ancient myths and legends, such as the tales surrounding Woolpit. The stories of Woolpit, of a village where children reportedly appeared with unusual features and spoke an unknown language, have long intrigued researchers. The suspicion is that such tales might be rooted in actual encounters with advanced, possibly extraterrestrial entities or secret experiments that resulted in unexplained phenomena unfolding in isolated settings. These stories could be echoes of covert operations aimed at studying alien visitors or experimenting with genetic manipulation and dimensional portals. Governments might have sought to conceal evidence of these encounters to avoid political or social upheaval, especially if the stories hint at the existence of highly advanced beings or technologies that challenge current scientific understanding.

Some researchers propose that the mysterious Woolpit tales are not just local legends but the distorted remnant of real events involving secret military experiments or scientific projects. For example, a secret base hidden deep within land anomalies could have been the site of experiments involving the interaction between human and non-human entities, leading to the creation of legends about children with unusual traits or otherworldly appearances. These investigations might have involved manipulating local environments, creating anomalies or portals that allowed entities from other dimensions to interact with humans temporarily. The suppression of such stories could stem from a desire to keep sensitive projects under wraps, especially if they reveal technologies or biological research that would threaten established narratives or national security interests.

Ultimately, the possibility of secret investigations linked to Woolpit and similar tales suggests that some land anomalies might serve as cover stories for covert projects dealing with alien biology, dimensional gateways, or experimental zones. Therefore, it is useful for researchers interested in these mysteries to consider historical stories and legends as potential clues or remnants of past clandestine activities. Comparing documented anomalies with folklore can sometimes uncover patterns that point toward specific locations or technologies that are still classified today. Knowing these connections can help enthusiasts better understand the complexities surrounding unexplained land phenomena—possibly even guiding future investigations into hidden sites where history, science, and the unknown intersect in compelling ways.

13. ETHICAL AND CULTURAL IMPLICATIONS

IMPACT ON LOCAL COMMUNITIES

Legends about unidentified flying objects and mysterious encounters often leave a lasting imprint on the communities where these stories originate. These stories tend to become a core part of local identity, shaping how people see themselves and their environment. When a community becomes known for a particular close encounter or strange phenomenon, it fosters a shared sense of pride that can tie residents together across generations. Such legends often fuel local festivals, museums, and tours, turning what might seem like folklore into a source of pride and cultural uniqueness. Tourism naturally follows —people come from far and wide, eager to see the sites connected to these stories or to experience the local atmosphere enriched by decades of tales. This influx of visitors can inject new economic vitality into the area, boosting small businesses, hospitality industries, and craft markets. Over time, these legends transform the landscape, coloring everything from local architecture to the names of landmarks, creating a psychic map that continues to attract curiosity and engage residents with their cultural narrative.

As these stories circulate, they also influence societal responses over the years. In some communities, the presence of a legendary sighting validates local traditions or beliefs, embedding a sense of the mystical or even supernatural into everyday life. Others might respond with skepticism, viewing these stories as harmless folklore or tourism tools rather than genuine phenomena. Yet, the real impact happens when these tales influence generations, shaping attitudes toward the unknown. Sometimes, local schools and scholars investigate these legends, trying to understand their origin or cultural significance, which adds academic legitimacy. In some cases, resident groups or local authorities organize events or festivals commemorating these encounters, fostering unity and collective identity. Regardless of the stance, these legends often become a way for communities to respond to broader societal influences—becoming symbols of resilience, curiosity, or even resistance against mainstream narratives that dismiss their stories as mere myth.

CULTURAL NARRATIVES AND IDENTITY

Stories like Woolpit serve as more than mere tales; they shape how cultures understand and interpret the unknown. These narratives often feature mysterious beings, strange lands, or unexplained phenomena that challenge everyday reality. Over time, such stories become woven into the fabric of cultural myths, influencing perceptions not just about their specific content but about what is considered possible or real. For example, tales of Woolpit, with its strange green children and otherworldly elements, evoke a sense of wonder and curiosity while also reinforcing cultural identities that embrace mystery or the supernatural. These stories act as cultural anchors, giving communities a shared sense of history and a framework for understanding the strange or unexplained events that defy conventional logic.

The power of these narratives extends beyond entertainment. They often serve as cautionary tales or social commentaries, subtly reflecting societal values, fears, or hopes. By framing the unknown through stories like Woolpit, cultures can explore themes of alienation, difference, or transformation. Such stories tend to resonate deeply, especially among groups interested in phenomena that seem to defy explanation, such as UFO encounters or alien sightings. They also help keep the conversation about the unexplained alive, framing it within a cultural context that lends familiarity and significance to these mysteries. This blending of myth and identity creates a collective memory, one that influences how subsequent generations interpret reports of strange sightings or encounters with the unfamiliar.

In the context of UFO research and popular culture, these myths act as a double-edged sword. On one hand, they foster a fertile ground for open-minded exploration and curiosity about the unknown. On the other hand, they can also reinforce misconceptions or unfounded beliefs if taken at face value without critical analysis. Recognizing the role of stories like Woolpit in shaping cultural perceptions is crucial. They are not just idle tales but powerful tools that influence societal reactions to unexplained phenomena. By understanding how such narratives embed themselves into cultural identity, UFO enthusiasts and researchers can better comprehend the emotional and psychological landscape in which these stories flourish. Whether these tales serve as explanations, warnings, or symbols, their impact on collective consciousness remains significant, guiding how communities perceive the mysterious.

Discussing ethical responsibilities, it's essential for those involved in preserving or debunking myths to navigate this terrain carefully. While myths and stories provide cultural richness, they can also perpetuate false beliefs or hinder scientific progress if not handled with integrity. Ethical considerations should guide efforts to document, analyze, or challenge these narratives, ensuring respect for cultural origins while also promoting critical thinking. For instance, when addressing stories like Woolpit, researchers must balance acknowledging their historical and cultural significance with the need for factual accuracy, especially in communities where these tales form a core part of identity. Debunking myths should not be about dismissing cultural expressions but about fostering a nuanced understanding that respects tradition while encouraging rational investigation. This responsible approach helps prevent the spread of misinformation and preserves the cultural fabric that stories like Woolpit help weave in.

In practical terms, engaging with these narratives requires sensitivity and ethical awareness. For UFO enthusiasts, this could mean clearly distinguishing between myth and evidence when discussing stories of alien encounters or strange phenomena. It also involves being transparent about the limits of current scientific understanding and recognizing the cultural value of these stories in shaping perceptions. Encouraging communities to maintain their folklore while embracing scientific inquiry fosters a healthy balance. Ultimately, the stories we tell about the unknown become part of our collective self-understanding, and handling them with care can nurture curiosity without sacrificing credibility. Knowing the origin and cultural significance of myths allows researchers and enthusiasts alike to participate in a dialogue that respects history while promoting a rational approach to unexplained phenomena.

ETHICS OF INVESTIGATION AND DISCLOSURE

When exploring phenomena that defy straightforward explanation—such as UFO encounters or unexplained sightings —researchers face a maze of moral questions. One fundamental consideration is how to approach these mysteries responsibly. It's tempting to prioritize uncovering the truth at all costs, but history shows that rushing to reveal every detail without careful thought can cause harm. A key aspect is respecting the privacy and well-being of witnesses, especially when their accounts are sensitive or could lead to social stigma. Additionally, the moral weight of possibly exposing sensitive government or corporate secrets must be balanced against the public's right to know. The core challenge lies in navigating between the desire for transparency and the potential consequences of revealing classified or dangerous information. Every revelation, even those fueled by curiosity, carries the risk of unintended repercussions, making it vital for investigators to weigh the ethical implications of every step they take.

In this landscape of mysteries, the debate over transparency versus secrecy grows fiercer with each new discovery. Supporters of openness argue that unexplained phenomena deserve honest discussion and public awareness, emphasizing that secrecy breeds distrust and suspicion. Keeping secrets can lead researchers and authorities into a murky world where misinformation flourishes, and the public becomes more anxious or suspicious. Conversely, defenders of secrecy point out that premature disclosures might cause panic, unease, or even interfere with national security interests. This tension is not new; throughout history, governments and organizations have often kept information under wraps to avoid chaos or maintain control. Yet, in the digital age where information spreads rapidly and skeptics are always ready to scrutinize, the balance tilts toward disclosure—though carried out with caution. Striking the right tone involves honesty about what is currently known, along with an acknowledgment of the limits of certainty. It's a delicate dance: being transparent enough to foster trust, while withholding sensitive details that could be misused or cause harm.

Practically speaking, moral investigation involves setting clear guidelines and standards for handling data and sources. Investigators should prioritize truthfulness, avoid sensationalism, and stay mindful of the potential impacts of their disclosures. This can mean establishing protocols that include double-checking facts, respecting witness privacy, and considering the broader social consequences before releasing information. Transparency doesn't necessarily mean revealing everything all at once; it can involve sharing verified findings gradually, accompanied by context that helps the public understand the limits of current knowledge. For researchers, developing an ethical framework that emphasizes honesty, responsibility, and sensitivity is crucial. Always remember that in the realm of unexplained phenomena, trust is built on integrity. Sharing information responsibly helps prevent sensationalism and ensures that investigations contribute to a more informed, less anxious community of enthusiasts and skeptics alike. Ultimately, maintaining ethical standards guides not just what is revealed, but also how it shapes public perception and ongoing inquiry.

14. SCIENTIFIC BREAKTHROUGHS AND FUTURE RESEARCH DIRECTIONS

EMERGING TECHNOLOGIES AND DETECTION METHODS

New tools like drone surveillance, spectral analysis, and advanced AI algorithms are turning the tide in the search for answers about mysterious phenomena. Drones have become more than just remote-controlled aircraft; they now serve as high-tech eyes in the sky, capturing footage from angles and heights impossible for humans. These flying devices can hover silently over remote or difficult terrains, providing real-time footage and sensor data that might reveal details often missed by traditional patrol or observation methods. When equipped with infrared and thermal cameras, drones can detect subtle temperature variations, potentially uncovering hidden objects or unusual activity even in low-light or obscured conditions.

Spectral analysis pushes the boundaries of what technology can do for researchers hoping to identify unknown signals or materials. By examining the light spectrum emitted or absorbed by objects, spectral analysis can distinguish between natural and unnatural substances, identify chemical compositions, or detect unusual energy emissions. This technique has already found success in fields like astronomy and archaeology, and now it's being adapted for investigating unexplained aerial phenomena. Coupled with sensitive sensors, spectral analysis can help locate anomalies in areas that seem ordinary, potentially unlocking clues about objects or phenomena that defy natural explanation.

Meanwhile, AI algorithms are becoming essential tools for making sense of the vast amount of data collected through these technologies. Machine learning systems can analyze images, signals, and sensor readings faster and more accurately than humans, spotting patterns that would otherwise go unnoticed. For instance, AI can sift through thousands of hours of drone footage to identify unusual movements or shapes that might indicate the presence of something extraordinary. It can also help filter out natural false positives, such as birds or weather phenomena, focusing only on data points that warrant closer inspection. As AI continues to develop, its ability to recognize and categorize unidentified objects or signals will become increasingly sophisticated, opening new pathways to understanding long-standing mysteries like Woolpit's strange sightings.

All of these emerging detection methods are not just about collecting data; they're about transforming raw information into meaningful insights. For enthusiasts and researchers keen on unraveling the unknown, mastering the use of drones equipped with thermal cameras, spectral sensors, and AI analysis tools can turn the tide in investigations. The key is to stay updated on the latest tech developments and learn how to combine different tools for a comprehensive approach. For example, deploying drones with spectral sensors during a sighting event can pinpoint abnormal energy signatures, while AI can interpret the footage in real-time, alerting investigators instantly to anything unusual. When you integrate these methods into your investigations, you greatly improve the chances of capturing and understanding phenomena that once seemed impossible to explain.

Adapting to these technological advancements also means being prepared to analyze new types of data. This involves developing an understanding of spectral signatures, sensor calibration, and the capabilities—and limitations—of AI systems. Regularly updating your equipment and software ensures you're working with the most effective tools. Establishing protocols for drone deployment, data collection, and analysis can help streamline investigations, making it easier to react quickly when a potential sighting occurs. Remember, the success of these technologies depends on both proper deployment and interpretation, so taking the time to learn their nuances will give you an edge in solving mysteries like Woolpit's strange lights or unexplained aerial events.

Always keep in mind that the combination of these tools can uncover hidden clues others might miss. For example, spectral analysis can reveal chemical traces suggesting the presence of unfamiliar materials, while drones can capture atmospheric conditions at different altitudes. When paired with AI-driven analysis, the chances of accurately identifying or ruling out natural explanations increase significantly. Whether it's a sudden flash of light or a strange object hovering silently, having a multifaceted technological approach increases the likelihood of gathering definitive evidence, helping turn speculation into solid understanding. Staying informed about emerging tech is crucial for any serious researcher committed to cracking the secrets behind UFO sightings, mysterious signals, or even historical enigmas like Woolpit's strange stories.

INTERDISCIPLINARY APPROACHES TO UNSOLVED MYSTERIES

One of the most promising ways to approach unsolved mysteries in the realm of unidentified phenomena is through bringing together professionals from varied backgrounds. Imagine scientists, ufologists, historians, and paranormal investigators sharing their insights and methods. Each group brings a unique perspective: scientists offer technical expertise on physics and instrumentation, ufologists contribute specialized knowledge about sightings and patterns, historians provide context by connecting clues to past events, and paranormal experts explore the less tangible aspects that might be overlooked by conventional science. When these experts collaborate, they can cross-validate findings, challenge assumptions, and uncover connections that might have remained hidden if they worked separately. Such teaming up fosters a more comprehensive understanding and opens the door for breakthroughs that no single discipline could achieve alone.

Building effective partnerships requires establishing open communication channels, creating shared goals, and respecting each discipline's approach. For example, scientists might develop new detection instruments, while ufologists can help interpret sightings data, and historians can identify patterns over centuries. The key is to create a dialogue where each expert recognizes the value of others' contributions. Regular meetings, joint field missions, and shared databases make collaboration more fruitful. When diverse minds unite around a common question, the resulting insights can be surprisingly profound, revealing aspects of mysteries that might have remained unexamined in isolated efforts. This approach not only enhances credibility but also accelerates the pace of discovery, inspiring new pathways of inquiry.

A comprehensive approach to unexplained phenomena involves looking at the problem from multiple angles simultaneously. Instead of focusing only on collecting visual evidence or eyewitness accounts, a holistic strategy integrates physical data, historical context, psychological factors, and cultural influences. For instance, when investigating a strange aerial sighting, researchers might deploy high-tech sensors to record electromagnetic fluctuations, analyze the physical environment for anomalies, and consult historical archives to uncover past incidents in the area. Gathering eyewitness testimonies helps to understand personal perceptions, while examining psychological factors explains potential misinterpretations or psychological influences on sightings. Such an all-encompassing method reduces the risk of tunnel vision and increases the likelihood of uncovering genuine anomalies.

This strategy calls for the creation of multidisciplinary teams that work together throughout the investigation. For example, a team might include engineers, psychologists, historians, and field researchers, each contributing insights across their expertise. Utilizing a variety of tools—such as electromagnetic sensors, atmospheric analyzers, and historical records—allows for cross-referencing data. This integrated approach also encourages developing theories that account for different influences, preventing premature conclusions based on incomplete data. Ultimately, a holistic framework enhances the credibility of findings and provides a richer understanding of complex mysteries, enabling researchers to piece together clues that may seem disconnected at first glance but are mutually illuminating when viewed together.

POTENTIAL FOR
NEW DISCOVERIES

Future research has the power to reshape how we see the legends and stories that have been passed down through generations. As technology advances, investigators are increasingly able to uncover details that were previously hidden or misunderstood. For instance, high-resolution imaging, thermal cameras, and data analysis tools enable us to examine historical sightings and artifacts with a new level of precision. This might lead to confirming whether certain mysterious objects or phenomena were truly unexplained or if they can now be explained through scientific means. Every new discovery adds a layer of depth to our understanding, sometimes confirming age-old beliefs but other times completely flipping what we thought we knew. As researchers remain patient and meticulous, there's a real chance that long-held assumptions about certain legends will be either validated or debunked, opening the door to fresh insights.

Then there's the exciting prospect of groundbreaking scientific or paranormal revelations. Advances in physics and biology sometimes challenge our current understanding of reality, hinting that phenomena once considered supernatural or inexplicable might have scientific explanations waiting to be uncovered. Imagine, for example, that new sensory or measurement technologies reveal that strange lights observed in the sky possess a form of energy or particles we haven't yet identified. Or that unexplained sounds or sensations linked to certain locations might be connected to undiscovered natural forces or even unknown life forms. These revelations could redefine the boundaries of science and turn some paranormal mysteries into scientifically provable facts. The thrill lies in the unknown, for as breakthroughs emerge, long-standing mysteries become not just stories but testable facts.

Progress hinges on curiosity, collaboration, and openness to new ideas. As new tools are developed—such as quantum sensors, deep-space probes, or AI-driven data analysis—we gain access to realms of information that were once out of reach. These innovations can lead us to discover anomalies or signals that defy current understanding, stirring excitement among enthusiasts and scientists alike. For example, the detection of unusual particle bursts, unexplained radio signals, or even direct observations of phenomena that previously only existed in reports or folklore can ignite a new wave of research. Regularly revisiting old cases with fresh eyes or methods might yield new clues, and open-minded exploration remains essential. Remember, the next breakthrough might just appear from a fresh approach, an unexpected connection, or even a lucky coincidence, sparking discoveries that could redefine the entire field of unidentified phenomena.

15. THE MYSTERY OF THE GREEN CHILDREN: REASSESSMENT

HISTORICAL
REEVALUATION

Reevaluating popular legends often involves uncovering fresh evidence or applying modern analytical techniques to old data. As time goes on, new archaeological discoveries or declassified documents can shed light on stories long considered myths. For instance, recent examinations of ancient texts or artifacts sometimes reveal details that contradict or deepen our understanding of the narratives surrounding mysterious phenomena. When researchers revisit these legends with contemporary tools—like advanced dating methods or spectral analysis—they often find inconsistencies or clues that were previously overlooked.

One striking example involves ancient artwork or inscriptions that depict sky phenomena. Historically dismissed as allegories or misunderstandings, these depictions take on new significance when examined with a fresh perspective or scientific scrutiny. Sometimes, reinterpretations emerge from a wider contextual understanding of the culture and its beliefs at the time, leading to a reconceptualization of the legend. Updated evidence can fundamentally shift the way enthusiasts and researchers perceive certain sightings or stories, transforming them from mere folklore into plausible encounters documented by earlier civilizations.

Furthermore, reinterpretations also emerge from challenging long-held assumptions about the authenticity of sources. Old chronicles or eyewitness accounts are scrutinized, with new criteria applied to assess their reliability. For example, some stories once dismissed as fabrications may, upon rigorous validation, reveal patterns consistent with known phenomena like plasma activity or atmospheric anomalies. This process often involves cross-referencing legends with independent data sets, such as climate records or celestial event logs, to establish correlations. These new insights can reshape the entire narrative, shifting the legend from folklore to a historical record worthy of serious investigation.

Legendary stories don't remain static over centuries—they adapt, grow, and embody the cultural currents of their times. As civilizations evolve, so do the narratives they tell. For instance, a sighting of an unexplained aerial object in ancient times might have been interpreted through the lens of divine intervention, often related to gods or spirits. As religious beliefs shift or scientific understanding advances, these stories transform, sometimes losing their divine context and morphing into tales of mysterious devices or intraterrestrial visitors.

Throughout history, cultural shifts have also influenced how legends are passed down. Oral traditions, for example, tend to change details each time a story is retold, subtly aligning with the listener's worldview or societal norms. When a legend traverses different regions or cultures, it often adopts new symbolism and significance, which modifies the core story over time. A story about mystical lights could be reinterpreted as flying ships or extraterrestrial crafts, depending on the society's prevailing technological or spiritual beliefs. These adaptations help the legend survive, ensuring it resonates with successive generations while reflecting their understanding of the world.

In recent decades, the rise of modern technology and media has dramatically influenced this evolution. Films, books, and internet stories shape contemporary versions of traditional legends, often amplifying certain themes or adding sensational details. Such portrayals can reinforce beliefs or introduce new elements, encouraging a cyclical reinforcement of the myth. Over time, this evolution can lead to a layered, complex understanding that blends ancient accounts with modern interpretations, making the phenomenon appear timeless yet continually reshaped by cultural currents. Recognizing this ongoing process helps researchers differentiate between original observations and modern embellishments, providing a clearer view of how legends evolve but still carry echoes of past encounters.

CONNECTION TO UFO AND ALIEN PHENOMENA

Throughout history, many legends and stories have been linked to strange sightings in the sky, often involving mysterious lights, crafts, and beings that defy our understanding. These tales seem to resonate across cultures and continents, suggesting a universal fascination with objects or entities that appear beyond human technology or natural phenomena. When examining global UFO encounters and alien sightings, it becomes evident that certain patterns emerge—bright, unusual lights often appear suddenly, moving with impossible agility and speed. Witness testimonies from different parts of the world frequently describe similar behaviors: craft that hover silently, make sharp turns, or disappear without a trace, fueling notions that these sightings are connected to a broader, shared phenomenon rather than isolated events.

Many researchers believe that these stories could point to encounters with intelligent extraterrestrial beings or, alternatively, highly advanced terrestrial technologies that remain hidden from mainstream science. The consistency in these reports challenges skeptics to dismiss them as mere hallucinations or fabrications. Instead, skeptics and believers alike are compelled to consider whether these accounts might be glimpses into regular contact with alien civilizations, whether through craft visiting from distant worlds or some form of unseen communication. The idea that a global phenomenon exists becomes even more compelling when recognizing the multitude of witness reports, documentation, and even government disclosures. All of these suggest that humanity's fascination and interaction with unidentified flying objects might be part of a larger framework of extraterrestrial contact that spans generations and borders, connecting stories from ancient cave paintings to modern radar tracking.

When connecting these legends to actual events, one interesting angle involves analyzing the environmental and social contexts. Many sightings tend to spike during times of societal upheaval, war, or major scientific breakthroughs, possibly reflecting collective subconscious fears and hopes. For example, during the Cold War, numerous secret military experiments were mistaken for UFOs, adding layers to the legend. However, some encounters defy rational explanation, such as eyewitnesses describing beings emerging from crafts or unexplained electromagnetic disturbances coinciding with sighting reports. This has led some to believe that these events are not merely misidentifications but manifestations of a relationship between humanity and non-human intelligences, whether they are visitors from distant stars or entities residing among us unnoticed.

Whether tied to ancient myths or cutting-edge reports, many stories have symbolic elements that seem to symbolize something beyond simple sighting. These legends can be seen as modern mythologies that embody collective dreams, fears, and curiosity about the universe and our place within it. Exploring these stories helps to understand the human tendency to attribute the unknown to higher powers or advanced civilizations that challenge our understanding of reality. Sometimes, these tales serve as warnings or messages, encoded with symbolism that resonates spiritually or culturally, hinting at a connection between extraterrestrial phenomena and divine or supernatural themes ingrained in human history.

Recognizing these patterns can help researchers identify recurring motifs and symbols that might point to deeper meanings or unresolved questions about the potential origins and intentions of these alien encounters.

THE GREEN CHILDREN AS INTERDIMENSIONAL BEINGS

The story of the Green Children of Woolpit has long intrigued skeptics and believers alike. Traditionally seen as a mysterious medieval legend about two children with green-tinted skin appearing in a small English village, recent theories propose a much more extraordinary explanation. Some researchers suggest that these children were not ordinary humans but travelers from a different realm, possibly from a parallel universe or an alternate dimension. This hypothesis gains traction when we consider certain unusual aspects of their story —such as their strange speech, their unfamiliar environment, and persistent reports of otherworldly qualities surrounding their origins. If we accept the idea that they might have come from a realm beyond our ordinary perception, it opens a fascinating door into the realm of interdimensional travel and the possibility that such phenomena are not just myth but rooted in realities we are just beginning to understand. This perspective challenges our conventional ideas about space, time, and reality, suggesting that the universe might be layered with hidden pathways connecting different worlds, accessible through unknown portals or gateways.

Connecting this idea to modern UFO and paranormal theories

reveals many striking similarities. Today's sightings often involve objects and entities that defy our understanding of physics, appearing suddenly and vanishing just as quickly. Many witnesses report encounters with beings that seem to exist outside our normal dimensions, sometimes described as interdimensional travelers or dimensional hitchhikers. These entities are said to manifest in our universe, only to slip back into their own realms, leaving behind a trail of confusion and wonder. The Green Children's story resonates strongly with these accounts, especially considering their otherworldly behaviors and appearances that don't precisely match any known human or animal traits. Some researchers believe these phenomena could be linked to hidden gateways embedded in the fabric of reality—portals that allow beings to move between different planes of existence. This idea aligns with recent discoveries in quantum physics and theories of multiple universes, where boundaries are not as firm as they seem and reality itself might be more layered than we've assumed.

Understanding the possibility that the Green Children were interdimensional explorers helps us reevaluate many ancient and modern mysteries. If they truly came from another realm, it suggests that what we consider impossible may just be unexplored science waiting to be uncovered. For those interested in this field, it's useful to consider that many strange sightings and encounters could be glimpses into these hidden pathways. Keeping an open mind and examining evidence through this lens may lead to breakthroughs in understanding other phenomena, such as crop circles, unexplained lights, or even the origins of certain folklore. Paying attention to anomalies in the environment, especially those that seem to appear or disappear without explanation, might clue us into where these bridges between worlds are located. Such approaches underscore the importance of integrating both ancient stories and cutting-edge science to deepen our grasp of the universe's true nature and the potential that interdimensional travel could be more than just fiction.

16. FINAL THOUGHTS: CONVERGENCE OF LEGENDS AND EVIDENCE

SYNTHESIZING MYTH AND MODERN SCIENCE

Throughout history, stories of strange lights, mysterious objects, and encounters with unknown entities have been part of human culture. Ancient civilizations often recorded phenomena that seem remarkably similar to modern UFO sightings, from the swirling lights mentioned in ancient texts to the strange crafts described in medieval illustrations. These accounts, often dismissed as myth or superstition, can be viewed as the earliest observations of genuine phenomena that still puzzle researchers today. As scientific methods developed, scholars began to analyze these stories more systematically, searching for patterns or explanations that could fit into an empirical framework. While early scientific inquiry often discounted the supernatural or unproven, advances in technology have now allowed us to revisit these ancient accounts with a fresh perspective. Modern-day discoveries— such as high-resolution satellite imagery or sophisticated radar —offer tangible evidence that can corroborate some of these oldest stories. By combining these historic narratives with the latest scientific data, a clearer picture emerges of how unexplained phenomena might fit into our universe's mysteries. This synthesis not only respects the curiosity of our ancestors but also broadens our understanding of what could be possible beyond conventional explanations, linking the stories of old with discoveries made in recent decades.

Highlighting the ongoing dialogue between legend and empirical inquiry means recognizing that these two worlds are not always separate. Legends often serve as cultural memory, passed down orally or in written form, carrying clues about phenomena that our ancestors could observe but lacked the scientific vocabulary to describe. Today, researchers compare these stories with data from telescopes, aircraft radar, and aerial surveillance to seek common threads. For instance, many ancient cultures describe sky disc or flying objects that resemble modern shape-shifting crafts or luminous disks. Scientific investigation doesn't aim to dismiss these accounts as mere myth but rather to consider whether they might be metaphorical descriptions of real phenomena that were poorly understood at the time. The ongoing discussion encourages researchers to remain open-minded and resourceful, using historical accounts as a starting point for investigation, while employing modern tools to decipher the nature of what was observed. With each discovery, the boundary between myth and science becomes less rigid, opening the door to new interpretations and possibilities. As legendary stories get examined under the light of current technology, they could reveal insights into atmospheric anomalies, unidentified aerial objects, or even undiscovered natural phenomena that align with tales from centuries past.

Integrating these two viewpoints—myth and science—is essential for a full understanding of mysterious phenomena. When historic accounts and modern scientific findings are examined side-by-side, patterns often surface that are otherwise overlooked. For example, many sightings of strange lights around certain geographical locations have persisted through generations, prompting scientists to investigate local environmental factors—such as unusual weather conditions, electromagnetic activity, or unique geological features—that could explain these recurring sightings. Similarly, explorations into ancient texts reveal descriptions that match phenomenons like plasma discharges or atmospheric optical effects, bringing tangible explanations to some long-standing stories. This approach acknowledges that both legend and empirical inquiry can inform each other, creating a more nuanced perspective on unexplained events. It encourages us to view old tales not solely as myths but potentially as encoded observations of natural phenomena or even unfamiliar technology. By weaving together historical records and scientific evidence, we develop a richer understanding that challenges the idea of unexplained phenomena as merely fantasy—sometimes, they could be echoes of discoveries waiting to be confirmed by science.

WHAT THE WOOLPIT TALE TELLS US ABOUT UNEXPLAINED PHENOMENA

Humans have always been captivated by the unknown. From ancient legends to modern reports of strange lights in the sky, there's a deep-rooted desire to understand what lies beyond our normal experiences. The story of Woolpit, with its strange green children and mysterious origins, captures that timeless curiosity perfectly. Such tales stir our imagination and prompt questions about the nature of reality, consciousness, and the universe itself. They remind us that some phenomena remain elusive, often defying logic and scientific explanation, which only fuels our drive to search deeper for answers.

This fascination with unexplained phenomena is not limited to folklore or legends but extends into modern-day sightings and encounters. UFO sightings, mysterious sounds, or inexplicable lights challenge our understanding of physics and the universe. For many, these stories evoke a sense of wonder and sometimes fear, but they also inspire scientific inquiry and speculation about life beyond Earth. These mysteries often serve as a reflection of humanity's innate curiosity, a quest to expand what we know and confront the boundaries of our knowledge. Engaging with these stories encourages us to ask difficult questions about our place in the cosmos and whether others may share our universe.

The tale of Woolpit demonstrates how legends and folklore act as gateways to exploring the unexplained. While the story itself might seem fantastical—green children appearing in medieval England—it mirrors the kinds of phenomena people continue to encounter today. As with modern reports of unidentified flying objects or strange creatures, stories like Woolpit ignite intrigue and motivate people to look beyond the obvious. They serve as symbolic representations of mysteries waiting to be investigated, pushing both enthusiasts and researchers to consider possibilities that challenge established scientific norms.

Legends like Woolpit also encourage the exploration of cultural perspectives on the unexplained. Every society has stories that involve mysterious beings, phenomena, or unexplained events, reflecting a universal tendency to interpret the mysterious through stories handed down through generations. These narratives often contain clues—metaphors, symbolism, or cultural anxieties—that can inspire scientists and explorers to question assumptions and look for unconventional explanations. Sometimes, legends act as early warnings or warnings disguised as stories, hinting at unexplored phenomena that modern science can investigate further.

For UFO enthusiasts and researchers, stories such as Woolpit emphasize the importance of maintaining an open mind. While skepticism is healthy, dismissing legends outright can hinder discovery. Instead, examining these tales critically, considering possible explanations—ranging from misunderstood natural events to potential encounters with unknown entities—can open new pathways for investigation. In a way, legends act as shared cultural touchpoints, reminding us that the universe still holds many secrets, and our curiosity should remain unbounded as we seek to uncover what truly lies beyond our current understanding.

THE ONGOING QUEST FOR TRUTH

Throughout history, humans have been driven by an innate curiosity about the unknown. When it comes to UFOs and unexplained phenomena, this curiosity fuels a relentless desire to uncover the truth. Enthusiasts and researchers often find themselves glued to accounts, sightings, and data that challenge conventional understanding. This pursuit isn't just about collecting stories; it involves applying scientific methods —questioning, testing, and verifying—to sift through countless reports and separate genuine encounters from illusions or misinterpretations. The process requires patience and an open mind, as sometimes the most compelling evidence emerges from unexpected sources. Keeping that curiosity alive, even when faced with dead ends or skepticism, is what sustains this quest for truth over time.

Accurate investigation hinges on combining factual inquiry with a skeptical but open attitude. As new information surfaces, it's crucial to scrutinize it carefully, evaluate sources, and consider alternative explanations. Scientific rigor becomes essential—using tools such as environmental analysis, radar tracking, and photographic authentication to validate sightings. Applying persistent curiosity involves asking probing questions. What patterns emerge from the data? Are there commonalities in sightings across different regions and times? Can the reported phenomena be explained by human-made objects, natural events, or other known factors? This discipline turns raw reports into credible evidence, advancing the broader understanding of unidentified phenomena. Such investigations often lead to new questions, reinforcing the idea that the search itself is as meaningful as the answers uncovered.

This unending search for answers remains a fundamental aspect of human nature, especially among those fascinated by the mysteries of the universe. The allure of the unknown taps into a primal instinct—an urge to comprehend things beyond our immediate perception. For many enthusiasts, the act of questioning becomes an animated pursuit of truth, where each new sighting or anomaly ignites further curiosity. It's not just about finding definitive proof but about continually challenging what we think we know and pushing the boundaries of understanding. This process helps keep the field alive and vibrant, encouraging new generations to look upward with wonder and skepticism alike. Sometimes, the investigation becomes a community effort, where shared experiences and collaborative analysis deepen the overall quest, making it a collective human endeavor powered by curiosity and a desire to know what lies beyond our ordinary senses.

By Patrick Gunn

Printed in Dunstable, United Kingdom